The New Earth

The New Earth

250 Billion Years AD

MICHAEL JESWEAK

Order this book online at www.trafford.com
or email orders@trafford.com

Most Trafford titles are also available at major online book retailers.

This is a work of fiction. All of the characters, names, incidents,
organizations, and dialogue in this novel are either the products
of the author's imagination or are used fictitiously.

Printed in the United States of America.

ISBN: 978-1-4269-5882-3 (sc)
ISBN: 978-1-4269-5881-6 (e)

Trafford rev. 02/15/2011

 www.trafford.com

North America & international
toll-free: 1 888 232 4444 (USA & Canada)
phone: 250 383 6864 ♦ fax: 812 355 4082

Chapter One

Hi. My name is Orian Grant, and I want to tell you a story about a great adventure I had when I left on a fifteen-story starship with my dad, my two brothers, and three of our close friends. We were searching for life on another planet where humans and animals could live. My friends and me and Doc—Dr. John Grant—were the only ones who took the long journey, and we were put to sleep until the spaceship found a planet that would support life.

The fifteen-story starship is the *Grant*. It was programmed by Doc to search for new life on different planets in our solar system; somewhere among all those stars and solar systems, he knew there must be life. At least Doc, my father, always thought so. And I think most people believed that deep down as well.

There were seven of us on this huge ship. It is nearly three football fields long and just as wide. This spaceship was sitting on our farmland even as Doc worked for NASA.

I have two brothers. Luke is fifteen years old, and he has a girlfriend named Beth. She is also fifteen years old. My other brother and the nerd of the family is Shane. He is sixteen years old, and his girlfriend Amanda is too. My girlfriend Doreen and I are both seventeen years old.

Then there is the man who made everything possible to begin a new life and to preserve mankind: Doc Grant. He had us start over on a near earth-like planet. Luke, Shane, and I were raised by our father, Dr. John Grant, or Doc as we called him. Our mother, however, died while giving birth to Luke. One thing that none of us planned on was waking up by a beautiful new world later than 250 billion years AD.

We lived in the country on 120 acres just thirty miles from NASA, where Doc worked for most of his life. He was considered a genius by his peers in the scientific field. Doc was a *Star Trek* fan and a big fan of *Star Wars* as well. Doc was also a big believer in the technology that both Gene Roddenberry and George Lucas brought to the big screen, and Doc worked on that technology at his home lab. Doc made it possible to create great things with his mind. Projects he designed were things like NASA's space shuttles, the landing rovers that landed on Mars, and many other inventions that he brought not only to NASA but to the whole world.

Doc was a good provider for us. He used the millions of dollars that he made to work on his starship, along with his many new technologies and inventions.

Doc's radical ideas conflicted with his work at NASA. Doc tried to convince NASA that his inventions of light-speed propulsion engines for the future of space travel not only were possible but also had been proven in his lab. Doc invented artificial gravity for space travel and force fields. NASA laughed at his ideas and never ran his calculations or saw his working models. So Doc worked in his lab or on the spacecraft that he had been building for the past twenty years on our farm.

My brothers and friends and I went to a small school in the country in a town called Blossom, Florida. We all played together for most of our lives and were very close. My brothers and I were teased a lot, mostly because Doc was building a spacecraft of huge proportions—fifteen stories tall and three times the length of a football field—on the side of our farm, but we shrugged it off. Even though we agreed with our friends and schoolmates that this spaceship would never leave the ground or even work, we still loved Doc and encouraged him to reach for his dream. Our teachers always defended us by telling classmates that Doc had done enormous work on space travel in the past. Doc claimed to have made breakthroughs in lightspeed, gravity, force fields, and even launching probes into space using his so-called antimatter drives. They claimed Doc was a great man.

Over the years, our close friends and girlfriends would come to our house every day so they could to play in Doc's imaginary world. Luke was the one who clung to everything that Doc said and did. The rest of us would play in the huge ship that Doc was building. Doc created human-like robots called humanoids that would help us with our homework and help Doc build his ship.

On the weekends Doc would always make us listen to him try to explain why he was building a starship. Doc would tell us that everything that had happened in the past would happen again. Doc also believed that the Mayan calendar was correct that the world as we knew it would be destroyed in 2012 when all the planets and the sun would line up together.

Doc would tell us that some of the writings were true, but Doc believed that, when all the plants lined up, the planets' gravity would be so strong that all the planets' orbits would change around the sun; the outer planets would move closer to the sun. Then the sun's gravity would get so strong that Venus, Mercury, Earth, and Mars would be sucked into the sun with a big explosion, and Jupiter and Saturn would take the Earth's place in our solar system. Luke, Beth, Shane, and Amanda would listen to his ideas with amazement. Doreen and I would listen for a while, and then we would go and discuss where we were going to college.

As the years passed, Doc got fired from NASA. He was still making new inventions, and that enabled Doc to keep himself and our dream alive. NASA thought that Doc was not thinking in the present and in the space world called NASA; they wanted scientists who worked and thought with technology that had already been invented, and Doc was always looking light-years in the future.

Most scientists rejected his work and didn't believe in his new technology. But Doc still had friends in the scientific world, and they would let him tap into their super computers and compile all the data from geologists all over the world. They even tapped into the satellites in space to monitor the stars and our sun's behavior. He was always downloading any information off the internet—downloading anything and everything that he could get his hands on.

Late in the year 2011, Doc's monitors were picking up strong fireballs from the sun. We started having more earthquakes and volcanoes erupting than normal and a slight shift in the poles. But at last, Doc's spacecraft was finished. Doc went to our town meetings and told the people and even pleaded with them to consider coming with us to be saved from painful deaths. However, this made the townspeople very frustrated for years. People thought that Doc was nice but kind of crazy. Doc never gave up on all his friends and tried hard to get them to believe.

But the starship was filled to the brim with food, plant seeds, pigs, cattle, sheep, chickens, and almost everything that we eat to keep healthy. Doc had them in kind of strange-looking pods, and they looked like they were frozen in time.

Doc took me aside one day and said "Orian, someday you will have to be the head and captain of this ship and crew."

He took me to the bridge of the spacecraft and to a room down the hall and showed me the pods that he had created for us children and for some of our friends. I, Orian the disbeliever, was becoming a believer. I saw the readings coming from the sun and Earth on the computer screen and felt the small tremors underneath us. Doc had enough life pods for 1.050 people. He told me to tell my brothers and our friends to stay close to the craft.

My brothers Luke and Shane tried to convince their friends, and Amanda, Beth, and Doreen tried to convince their parents and friends to be ready to come when the alarm goes off, giving only an hour's notice before takeoff. We told everyone that they would be safe and welcome on the spaceship when the time came for the end of the Earth. Nobody except the six of us really believed that Doc was right.

The scientific world all said that everyone would be just fine and to just stay in their homes when we felt tremors and saw high tides. The governments of the world told coastal area residents to move inland due to higher than normal tides, rising sea levels, and plate movements. Still, they said everything would be fine if we just planned ahead of the alignment of the sun and the planets. All scientists agreed that there would be loss of life, but they said it would not be even close to a holocaust.

Doc talked in our small town on some TV stations and even showed the townspeople the data that his supercomputers had compiled. It just seemed like the more that Doc talked, the more the townspeople disbelieved. People would drive by and laugh at the large spaceship.

Other people loved its beauty. The starship, the *Grant*, was designed based on *Star Trek*'s *Enterprise* combined with the landing gear and design of a *Star Wars* attack ship and slim wings that Doc designed based on other movies, but the wings had robot arms in them that would be able to repair the ship if any damage came to it during flight. The starship could lift off the ground without a lot of rocket power, so Doc says.

Scientists around the world assured governments that the lining up of all the plants on December 21, 2012, would be a scary and intense moment for the believers of the Mayan calendar and the Bible, but not to worry—it would just be a bad day in some places. Some scientists predicted higher tides, more earthquakes, and that low-lying areas would suffer the worst while other people or cities that lived on faults on the earth's crust would have cause to be more worried. If only the world had known and had listened to my father about the ending of the earth and that all life would perish.

Whether the spaceship would work or not, my friends and I felt safe hanging around Doc and listening to him. The spaceship—or now Doc called it a starship—was beautiful, and we felt safe playing around it and learning about the *Grant*.

People stared as the huge letters stood out and were exposed. The letters were lit up at night for everyone to see. All would know that it was the world's best creation.

Doc loves his ship. The *Grant* was designed to lift up off the ground vertically and was able to travel at six times the speed of light or faster. The starship has a computer system that talks like a human and is able to make judgments. The computer also has emotions. The onboard computer takes care of all of the ship's functions. Our ship also has many humanoids that help with the ship and even create new materials from matter—even from space dust. The humanoids can work in space and fix any damages or change the ship's structure to meet or prevent future threats.

Beyond "Safety first," the starship's main objective is to find planets similar to Earth that could support life. NASA and others toured the *Grant*, but because it is such a large ship, NASA said that it would never leave the ground. Doc had faith in his ship. but we looked like a small crew.

It was then December 21, 2012, and Doc took new readings from the sun, the stars, and the Earth's plate movements. Things were getting worse day by day—floods, earthquakes, volcanoes in Florida, and Yellowstone National Park just exploded. Doc told Shane and me to go get our friends and get back as quickly as possible. First we stopped to pick up Dorcen, then Beth, and finally Amanda.

We told their parents what was happening, but they thought we were crazy and told us to just go and do what we had to do. They thought it was all nonsense, like everyone else in our town. No one would even think of coming on our starship, so it was just the seven of us going. The girls were crying about their parents and friends as we boarded the ship.

"Orian," Doc yelled, "get everyone strapped down. We have to take off now."

Luke and I helped everyone get strapped into our seats, which looked like pods. Then I had to tell Luke, the smart one, to strap in too, because I had to help Doc at the helm. The whole earth was shaking by then, and I could hear screams from the girls as water started to rise around us, coming up to the top of the helm of the starship. The ground was shaking, and the sky turned pitch black.

Doc started the computer's countdown, looked over and smiled at me, and said, "This starship is also waterproof." That is just Docs way; he's always calm.

The computer was counting down: five . . . four . . . three . . . two . . . one. Lift off!

The *Grant* started to rise off the ground and out of the water, and then we were off toward the heavens. There was no big jolt like the one Doc had expected.

"Orian," Doc said, "go and tell the others that they may come and watch."

I went into the pod units and yelled, "Doreen, are you okay?"

"Yes" she said.

Then Shane said "Okay, sir."

Beth yelled, "Is it over?"

The smart-alecky Amanda said, "Was that it? Boring!"

This was not the way that we had planned our adventure, which had begun.

When we got to the helm, Beth asked Doc, "Can we watch what is happening? I am so worried about my parents."

Amanda and Doreen asked as well.

"Yes," Doc told them.

"Aren't we now sixty million miles away from earth, Doc?"

"Yes, son, I told you that we have lightspeed and haven't even used it yet, but all of you," Doc said, "come and sit down, and I will open up the visual screen. Computer, open screen."

A big window appeared.

"We won't be able to see earth from this far away," Doreen said.

Doc laughed and said "Computer, magnify screen forty percent."

Soon the earth and sun and planets were all lined up like Doc had said they would be, and we could see the surface of the Earth as well as the other planets.

My father had sent out space probes quickly so we could record the end of the Earth and watch things unfold. Doc and the rest of my family and friends watched in terror the violent way that the earth disappeared forever on the viewer screen. We could hear the screams of people, and there was no way to help them without being destroyed. We had tried to warn them, but no one would listen to my father.

Some of the continents just sank into the sea. People were vaporized by the sun through cosmic waves, and the Earth was full of radiation. The Earth started to boil, and then all was quiet. As the planets slammed into the sun, they caused several explosions, and the sun seemed to grow more intense and larger. Our ship was bombarded with supernova-type impacts, but the shields held, and the starship stayed intact.

We all shed tears and hated what we saw. I felt sorry our friends on Earth. The girls wished their parents would have listened to Doc and gotten onto our beautiful ship. We watched the ever growing sun. Usually, when a sun or star grows that quickly, it means that the sun wouldn't have much time to live and would go supernova.

Even animals underground would be destroyed by the sun's radiation, and the weather will be on a rampage. The earth's crust would melt in the days and weeks ahead.

Over the years, Doc had shown NASA and other scientists his work on artificial gravity and other inventions that he had created. They had said that we were not advanced enough to design a working model of the project. Doc spoke in lectures at science events, and kids and adults alike said that our starship would not work or get off the ground. They said Doc's design for a new form of fusion engine or drive that would deliver speeds of six to seven times the speed of light would not work. NASA would never even consider Doc's ideas, and scientists all around the world said the world would realign and go back to normal in a few months.

As we watched for days and weeks, everything that Doc had said was going to happen did. We all cried as we watched the Earth and all the landmasses disappear.

"I can hear my mother crying in pain," Beth said.

Doreen gently took Beth and Amanda in her arms and said in a soft voice, "We all knew that this day would come. Let's just be happy that we have each other and thank Dr. Grant."

"No need for thanks, my young ones," Doc said. "That goes for you too, Orian, Shane, and Luke. I remember how it felt when my parents passed when I was at a young age and when I lost my wife. But they are still with us in our minds and hearts." Doc told the girls, "I wanted to borrow all of the videos your parents took while you were all growing up, and I made your family DVD copies."

"Yes," Amanda said.

"You didn't," Doreen said.

"Yes," Doc said. "All your history and family memories are on a secure hard drive that you can access any time you want."

"Great," we all said. "And thank you Doc."

Amanda asked Doreen what the future would bring to us. Doreen really didn't know, so we asked Doc.

"The first thing that we are going to do," Doc said, "is record the end of our solar system to remember. Then I will tell you and teach you what the future might be and what I hope it will to bring you."

So for about a month, we watched as Venus, Mercury, and then Earth slammed into the Sun, creating huge explosions and making the sun grow larger and brighter as the planets moved out of alignment. Mars was where Venus used to be.

After we watched the Earth blow up and get absorbed by the sun from a distance of sixty million miles, in just an instant, Jupiter came close to the sun, and Saturn and the rest of the planets got sucked into new orbits closer to our sun. Jupiter and Saturn were in the same orbit close to where the Earth used to be. The rest of the planets are all in weird orbits around our sun and closer.

Then Doc sat us all down and told us that he would leave a probe where we were then, and with his development of faster-than-light-speed video feeds, we would see if life reappeared on the surviving planets. Maybe we could come back some day. Doc's voice was raspy, and he told us that there had to be life somewhere in the universe among the billions of stars around us. His starship was designed to find life and keep sending out probes to search for life. We needed to find an Earth-like planet to be able to survive. Doc also told us about the pods that we would be hibernating in and that we would not age until we reached a planet that could support life.

"Then the computer will wake all of you up well beforehand and check for life-forms, air to breath, and gravity," Doc said. "But I have to tell you, you will probably never find another human again. Life on other planets will be foreign, maybe hostile."

Doc told all of us that the ship could last for millions of years or more and that we had everything on board to start a new life and to build homes. Doc took us to one of the cargo bays and showed us spacecrafts to use to fly around the new world and machines that we could work the ground with—so much we had to learn.

I asked Doc and he said that when he put us to sleep we would be tied into the computer system. It would constantly be updating all of the ship's features and our minds as we traveled. Doc also told us that he still had years of work to be completed and that he would not share with us in our sleep but would go on with his work.

"When will our journey begin?" Amanda asked.

"Now, my children," Doc said. "Come."

First he put a funny-looking band around Luke's head, and Luke asked what it was, Doc told all of us that it was our learning tool while we explored space.

"You shall all wear one," Doc said. Then he kissed Luke on the cheek and said "Sleep well, my darling Luke."

The pod closed, and Luke went to sleep.

"Now you, Beth." Doc also kissed her on the cheek and said, "Sleep well, my child." He told all of us that we are all one family now and to always remember home and be kind to one another. Then Beth's pod closed, and she was asleep.

"You're next, Amanda," he said, and the same for Shane.

"Come with me, Orian and Doreen," Doc said.

We went to the helm of the starship, and Doc showed us a chair with some buttons on it. Doc told Doreen and me that, when we found a world to live on and had landed on it, the chair would have the knowledge of the whole ship and of all the changes that the Doc and the computer would make over the years on the *Grant*.

"You both must take the knowledge that the chair has to offer and be both father and mother for the rest of our family."

Doc sat down and told the computer to search for worlds at propulsion speed of light by six. Then Doc told Doreen and me to go to our pods and get ready for our journey. As we were walking down to the pods, Doc told Doreen and me that he wouldn't be with us when we would find our new world. He said that, at our speed, time slowed down, and he would have many years to work on his new inventions. He told us that, only if he found a world before he passed on, would he see us again.

"Doc, no," I yelled.

Doreen was crying. "You can't, Dr. Grant."

"But I must," said Doc. "The future of our race is yours now. You know me, Orian; I have to work just so you chosen six will have a new beginning."

Then Doc put our memory bands on and kissed us, with tears running down his cheeks. Before he closed the pods his final words to us were that he loved us all the same—even the girls.

Chapter Two

I, Orian Grant, was the first one the computer woke up. I heard my father's words, saying, "Wake up, Orian. Time to start your journey." I heard it several times and finally woke up. I saw that the pod door was open, but only mine was. *Have I lost my brothers, friends?*

"Doc, is that you?" I yelled.

The computer responded that Doc had passed on, but I yelled "Doc, I can hear you."

The computer said, "Dr. Grant has programmed me to sound and act like him until you get oriented. I will then go to a default, bossy female voice."

I laughed, thinking to myself, *Wow, that sounds like Doc.*

"Orian, you can ask me anything. But first, Orian, sit in the chair that your father showed you before you went to sleep," the computer directed.

"Okay." I said.

My legs buckled under my weight, and my arms felt like Jell-O.

"Please come to your chair," the computer told me.

"Hold on," I yelled. "I can't walk. Why?"

The computer told me to call it Doc. It also told me that it remembered all the voices of the others.

"Okay, Doc, then why can't I walk?"

"Orian, you have been asleep for a very long time, and you will have to build your strength to get up and get moving about."

"What about the others?" I asked.

"They're just fine, Orian. After we get you moving and in the mind chair, then you can wake up your brothers and friends. They are just fine."

"Computer—Doc," I said. "Can you help me?"

"Hold on, Orian. I think that I can help you. One moment please."

Soon, two human-like robots arrived and slowly picked me up.

"Ouch. Not so hard," I told them.

"Sorry," one robot said, "Is this better, Orian?"

"Yes and thank you."

"We have to get you into the chair so that things will be much clearer."

The two robots put me in the mind chair and helped me to put on the device that Doc had created for Doreen and me to use.

It seemed like it took forever to get me to sit upright in the device that Doc had made for us. I kept slipping downward and asked Computer "What the heck is wrong with me? I still feel weak"?

"Hold on, Orian," the computer said. "I will reduce gravity levels in the ship so you and the others can gain your strength back."

Slowly, I was able to sit upright in Doc's special chair. The robots put a cap over my head, and the computer readied the process of knowledge expansion.

"Now what?" I asked. "I am strapped in and ready computer."

Soon I felt as if a bolt of lightning was hitting my head, and thoughts raced through my head—new thoughts and star systems and all of Doc's notes in the log, and I could feel Doc or the computer putting so much into my mind that I thought I was going to explode.

As soon as it started, it was over. My mind was full of knowledge. All of Doc's memories and inventions were mine to share with the others. I still couldn't wake them up yet.

The computer, or Doc as it wanted to be called, said, "Orian, you must take this new knowledge and put it to good use. I will walk you through everything step-by-step, but first, look in the mirror."

I looked in the mirror, and sure enough, I hadn't aged a day, just as Doc had said. I stumbled to the pods, my legs still unsteady, and looked at the others. All the lights on the pods were green, meaning that they were just fine. Everyone looked like they had that night Doc put us in our pods. It was like it was the night before. But my task wasn't over yet, and I had to wait until I checked out the new world while in orbit before I could awaken the others.

I didn't like to be alone at that fine of a moment, and losing Doc didn't help matters, so I decided to wake Doreen and put her in the chair as well. Then we would look at the new world together. I went to Doreen's pod and knew exactly what to do; that mind machine was fantastic. I told the computer to open Doreen's pod, and soon the door opened. She was still strapped in tightly and looking as beautiful as ever. I took her mind band off and then her straps. I saw that she was awake but a little bit confused. She just muttered the words, "Are we there yet?"

"I think so," I said to her.

I told Doreen about the chair. I also told her that she had to get up the strength to participate in the same way I had. Then we could share and see what the new world had to offer and make sure we can sustain life there.

Slowly, Doreen got up. She wobbled a bit, but since we had decreased gravity, she was able to get on her feet more easily—well, at least, more easily than I had. I told Doreen about Doc passing and about the computer wanting us to call it Doc. But it just didn't feel right.

"Computer," I said, "we can keep your voice, but I am going to just call you 'Computer,' the name you should have been called all these years."

"Yes, son, I will accept your decision, but will you consider calling me 'Doc' once in a while, the name your father gave me?"

"Okay," I said. "Then 'Computer' it is. But, Computer, sometimes when I get lonely and I talk to you at night, I may call you 'Doc.' Will you tell me space stories and stories of what we have left behind?"

"Yes, Orian, I would like that. Not just for you, but for Doreen, Luke, Shane, Beth, and Amanda as well."

Doreen sat in the chair that I had sat in and went through the same experience that I had gone through, but she giggled all the way through like she was on a joyride. I guess that's Doreen—always laughing, joking, and loving to learn. I thought to myself, *Maybe I should make her the boss . . . no way; she would love bossing me around too much.* I laughed to myself.

When she was through with the mind transformation, she cried and told me how she missed her family and talked about the loss of my father whom she and all of us had loved so dearly.

Doreen and I talked, and we decided to wake up the others. The ship had seven chairs sitting at the helm—one for each and every one of us, even my father. I asked Doreen to wake up Amanda and Beth. I said I would wake up Luke and Shane. We did one by one. They all woke up and stumbled to the floor. There were robots that looked like humans helping each and every one of them, just like they helped me.

Soon, we were all up and moving around the helm, getting a grip on things, learning how to walk and move our arms again. I asked the computer to decrease the gravity by another one percent, and just that little bit gave us our freedom back. I knew that we would have to slowly get our strength back in the workout room. I told the computer that, before we could set foot on the new world, it should increase the gravity a tenth of a percent every day until we reached Earth's gravity level again.

"Agreed," the computer said to us.

Doreen and I talked to the rest of the family—our new family—and decided that, when and if we landed in a world that we hadn't even seen yet, we would have to start putting the force fields up around the ship when we would farm, work, and start our new lives. For none of us knew what kind of life-forms, if any, were on the world.

We were all so young and scared, especially Shane and Beth. Luke was ready to get things going and go out on adventures as soon as we landed.

"We are all scared and have to remember the ones that were left behind and start a new life for each and every one of us," Doreen said, "so let's take this slowly."

Doreen and I told the younger ones, "Heck, we are all young, but the oldest has to lead just like in the past. Our first goal is to find out what this new world has to offer and if we can survive there." I told everyone to sit down so we could open the viewing screen.

I took over Doc's seat in the middle. Doreen sat on my right side, and Shane sat on my left with Amanda next to him. Beth and Luke sat at the other end. That left us with one chair empty and with all of our thoughts and memories going out to the great Dr. John Grant, or Doc as we all knew him by.

As we all sat in our seats, I said, "Computer, open screen," and as soon as those words were spoken, the screen opened up. There in the light of two suns we saw a huge blue world that was four times the size of Jupiter and that had at least four moons. One moon had purple rings around it, but there was no land in sight.

"Computer," I asked, "Why there is no land, and what is this planet's composition?"

"There is land here, Orian, and an Earth-like atmosphere." The computer said, and it went on to explain that the landmass is only half the size of Florida.

"How are we going to start a new life on this planet with such a small landmass on such a huge planet?" Doreen asked.

"As we grow in the future," the computer said, "we will be sending more probes into the universe. Be hopeful that we can adapt to this world while waiting for the return of our probes that we have sent out on this long journey. We are still receiving input from probes sent out over two hundred and fifty billion years."

"What?" I asked. "How long, Computer? How can this be?"

The computer answered, "Orian, even though it seems like a day to you and your friends, at the speeds your father was able to accomplish, time slowed down to a crawl. Still being on Earth time, my calculations show that, if the Earth had survived, it would have been two hundred and fifty billions years older."

"Why didn't we find a new world earlier?" Doreen cried out.

"Doreen, the universe has changed many times in all these years," the computer said. "With all of the new worlds that Doc found from probes sent out, we would get to our destination and the sun would go supernova on us or the new world just wasn't there anymore.

As we all sat in awe, Luke said, "Computer, take us to this landmass and let us see for ourselves."

"Is that okay, Orian?"

"Yes, Computer, take us there," I said.

Soon, we saw land, and the computer said, "We have arrived. I am searching for a good, solid landing site for the *Grant*. It seems that, in the center of this new continent, there is a great force generating from the center."

"Orian," Amanda said, "in the middle of that landmass is a crystal-like object with paths leading toward the mountains. When we land, we will have to see what the force is and find its source."

"Computer," I asked, "What is the purpose of this source?"

"Orian, this source is unknown. The oxygen level in this new world is greater than the Earth's."

"What more can you tell us about this new world?" I asked.

"My sensors tell us that, on this new world, the gravity is one percent lower than the Earth's gravity and that numerous vegetation have been detected, but all are unknown. The sea on this new world is freshwater and is abundant in organic material, and the fresh water world shows an abundance of freshwater creatures," said the computer. "Orian, I also detect that the average air temperature is eighty degrees."

As we all looked at the on-screen view of this beautiful blue-green planet, we decided this was the landmass that we would call home. As we looked closer at our new world, we noticed that this large planet had only the four moons we first saw. One looked similar to Saturn with its colorful rings; it looked like we could almost reach out and touch it. The beautiful moons of the new world seemed to share the same orbit. There was a beautiful, bright sun and multicolored clouds passed around the planet.

It was time to get ready to land on this beautiful, new planet we were about to call home.

As we continued to stare at the viewer screen, I said, "Doreen, Luke, do you see all those mountain ranges?"

"Yes" they replied. "They are so tall that they reach up to the sky all around the land."

"Yes, I see," Beth said.

"And look," said Amanda, "there are four openings to the sea below. That must be how the plants down on this new world get their water."

"Do you think that we can land now and see this new world?" Shane asked Doreen and me.

"What do you think, Computer? Is it safe to land?"

The computer checked the sensors again and said, "Yes, Orian. This land is firm and can hold the weight of the *Grant*."

"Let's find a nice solid, flat place to put down, Computer," said Orian.

"Your father would have been proud of all of you for being so brave," the computer said.

"Yes," Luke said. "When we touchdown, we can scan and check the ground ourselves."

"Good idea," Shane and Amanda said.

"I think I see a nice place to land," Luke yelled to me in excitement for touchdown.

"Looks perfect," Beth said. "Just hope that it will hold this huge starship's weight."

"Okay with you, Computer?" I asked.

"Seems stable enough to land the starship," the Computer said. "Take the helm, Commander Orian and see what you have learned."

"You sure, Computer?" I asked.

"Yes, commander, it is all yours," the computer said.

"Doreen, you help me with this task," I said.

"Okay, Commander Orian," she replied as she giggled.

I started the descent to our new home. The vertical thrusters were working just fine to make our descent an easy task. Our starship penetrated the atmosphere. I asked Doreen to activate the landing gear.

"Done," Doreen said.

I asked computer to slow our descent to half of a foot per second.

"Shane," I asked, "will you read off the countdown to landing please?"

"You bet, Orian," Shane said. "And here we go: Five. Four. Three. Two. One. Touchdown. The *Grant* has finally landed on our new home!"

"Well, guys," I said, "after two hundred and fifty billion years, this starship really needs to rest."

We all laughed.

"Now that we have landed," I continued, "it seems like it is getting dark out." I asked my brothers and friends if they would like to sleep now and get an early start in the morning.

"Well, whenever that comes," Luke said.

I told everyone that, while viewing the layout of the starship, I noticed that Doc and the computer had made many new changes to the ship, and they also created many new inventions.

"So tomorrow, you will take a section of the starship in the morning and explore the new modifications that Doc made," I said. I went on to say that I would go through the ship's logs, and Doc's memos to find out what we might encounter once we opened the ship's hatch. I needed to find a way to protect us against whatever we might encounter once we left the ship. "I'm sure Doc thought of those things as he was making new inventions and retrofitting the ship."

"Sounds like a plan," Shane and Luke replied.

We all went to our bedrooms and opened up our windows to look at the moons and the plant life on our new world. It was beautiful. The plant life on the planet had come alive. It all glowed with light green and bright orange and several shades of beautiful blue.

I went to Doreen's room and knocked on the door. I asked if she was awake.

"Is that you Orian?" Doreen asked.

"Yes," I said.

"Come on in, Orian," Doreen said.

"Can't you sleep, Doreen?" I asked with a gentle voice.

"No, I just have so much on my mind, Orian."

"Have you looked out your window? It is the most beautiful sight that I have ever seen."

"Yes, I have . . ." Doreen was overcome with sadness. I could tell that Doreen was holding back tears. "Oh, Orian, I miss my family, and I am sure the rest of the girls feel the same. It's not that I am ungrateful for what your father has provided for us, I just wish that more people would have listened to Doc and we could have saved more people."

I held Doreen and told her that the ship Doc had designed was for a group of fifteen thousand people.

"Doreen, I miss my father, friends, and even school," I said. "We will have to be strong for my younger brothers and their friends as well. I am going back to my room to think for a while and to try to get some sleep."

Doreen kissed me on the cheek and told me we had to make a lot of decisions the next day. I went back to my room and looked outside again. I asked the computer to turn the force field to 150 yards "just in case."

Before breakfast, I went to the helm and started going through Doc's computer files and video logs. I found out that our starship had landed on many planets to gather resources for Doc's new inventions. The computer had been gathering knowledge while we had gone forward in time. It was able to create anything new out of matter gathered—from space dust to other materials from different planets and moons. Doc created our ship and a computer system capable of creating objects with information he had imagined.

As I viewed more of Doc's logs, I realized that he had always known anything could be made up of atoms and formed into any matter that he chose. Before Doc's passing, the computer had been programmed to follow his mind in ways such as creating safe ways for us to live and to start a new life on a distant planet.

Luke and the others soon joined me at the helm. We were still in awe of the new world. We all wondered when we were going to live our lives and explore the new world. We all imagined what we would find.

Doreen finally told us that breakfast was ready. The computer had made us a great feast. As we were eating,

Luke told us that we should take inventory of the ship's cargo and see what changes our father had made.

"Good idea," I said to Luke. "After breakfast, we will take inventory of the ship's cargo, and I will keep listening to Doc's instructions in the log file."

Luke and Beth took the lower half of the ship, including the cargo bay. Shane and Amanda took the inventory of the middle of the ship. Doreen and I would meet up with Shane and Amanda and work on the upper decks together.

Luke and Beth started down the ship's elevator and reached the cargo bay. To their amazement, there were many different kinds of machines—everything from mining equipment to planting equipment, and even several machines that could travel both on the ground and in the air. Luke saw many other amazing machines. There were starships, weaponry, and many other things they were going to learn about. As Luke and Beth made their way up, floor by floor, they found sick bays and shuttle bays with many types of spacecrafts inside them.

Meanwhile, Shane and Amanda were searching the middle of the craft, and they found many empty rooms for more people to sleep in. That saddened them, because they couldn't save more people.

Shane walked into a large room, and yelled, "Amanda, come in here. You *have* to see this."

"What Shane?" Amanda asked.

In the room, they counted over one hundred human-like humanoids. They looked just like our family and friends and were all in separate tubes, just waiting for the time to be activated.

"Computer," Shane asked, "What is the purpose for all these humanoids?"

"To help with your protection and to help all of you build and explore your surroundings," the computer said.

"Cool," Amanda said.

While the rest of my brothers and friends explored the ship, I continued to view Doc's video logs and instructions. The logs told me most of what I need to know to start our new life and about how to construct new surroundings outside the starship. But somehow I knew most of it. I think I learned all of that information when I had sat in Doc's memory-enhancement chair.

I found belts that we were all supposed to put on when we ventured beyond the force field boundary and on our explorations. I discovered that the belts contained a built-in device for force fields for protection from weapons or alien attacks—just in case—plus small cell phone–like weapons for fighting in an attack. *Cool*, I thought. I couldn't wait to tell my brothers and friends about what I had found.

Later in the day, we were all at the helm. We started to talk about going outside to check out our new surroundings and take soil samples to see if we could plant seeds. We would also check out the plant life and set our outside force field to our liking and distance.

After Shane told me about the humanoids, I decided to activate them and have some of them put the force field in place while we worked on how to build our home outside. We also needed a place for aliens, if there were any, to communicate with us.

We already knew from the computer scans that the plant life here included forms of intelligent life. We would have to work with the plant life, and we would have to apologize for having destroyed any of them when we had landed.

There was just so much for us to do. We had to get ready to explore the planet and find out what that source of power in the center of the landmass was for and how we might be able to use it ourselves.

Chapter Three

"Well, it's time to leave the ship and start working on our new lives outside this ship," I said. "But remember, this will be our home until we can get a livable home outside. I asked Shane to go and activate some of the humanoids.

"Sure," Shane said.

I told Shane that they were numbered one through 150. Two of them had different suits on them. One was named Mark, and the other's name was Sue. The rest of them were numbered.

"So that is how we will address them," I continued. "Shane, just wake up twenty for now and give them instructions to start on the perimeter force field while we take samples of our surroundings. And also, Shane, the computer has loaded all the data from the ship to all the humanoids. I found out that they were all connected to the computer. We can ask them questions, and they will answer." The humanoids would do whatever we asked them to do, but I took Mark the humanoid as my personal one, and Doreen took Sue as her humanoid.

"They look so human and have emotions. Someday, we will name them all."

"Doreen, you work with me and help make plans. And Luke, since you like to fly and are really the smart one, you take one of the ships in the shuttle bay. For now, let the computer fly the ship with your commands until you get your wings. Beth, you go with Luke and keep him out of trouble."

We all laughed.

"Amanda, you help the humanoids start to construct a home for us. You have always been good at designs, and so is Doreen, so listen to what she says.

"You bet," Amanda said.

"When everyone's done, we will venture out and check the surroundings. And everyone, don't forget to strap on your protection belts. We will all take the first step outside in this new world as one," I said.

The time came for our group to take our first steps outside, and we all had to decide what to call our new world. I asked if everyone was ready to investigate outside, and everyone was truly excited.

"Let's go, people," someone said.

I pressed the button to open the cargo bay door. The door creaked and slowly opened. Then there it was: a beautiful place. The air smelled so refreshing. There was no smog or pollution, just clean, fresh-smelling air. We all held hands and took our first steps onto our new world.

The ground felt soft but firm. We would have to get used to the new gravity and get our strength back to be able to explore. Then we heard a loud noise as Luke and Beth took off in the sleek spacecraft the size of a large van. They zoomed around us and took off toward the mountains. We could see Luke's large smile. He waved as he took off into the unknown.

Shane gave the humanoids instructions on the size of the force field he wanted around the ship and where he wanted the fields for our future livestock. The humanoids went back into the cargo bay and started bringing out some tall, thin, rod-like objects. They kind of looked like our electronic fence rods from back home on the farm, but they were larger. The humanoids were hard workers, and they quickly started building the force field. They were careful not to hurt or damage the plants.

"We have to be careful until we can understand them," I said. "Because all of them might be intelligent; we just don't know yet. One never knows what kind of new life-forms these are, and they could be just as smart as or smarter than we are." I told everyone that Doc had trained our minds while we were asleep. We were given the ability to read minds with a device that we could wear in our ears. Just in case we encountered alien life or any other kind of life, we would have to practice what we learned from Doc and the computer.

"Weird," Doreen said.

Everyone started on the tasks assigned to them. We would all be inputting our individual information into the computer. We are all family now, even though I am the oldest and the one in charge. Everyone seems interested in different projects, so everyone has input on what needs to be done and how. That way we would avoid conflicts with one another by not getting in their way while we all built a new life on the planet.

One thing we noticed on the planet was that one day was approximately twenty to twenty-five days on Earth, as far as we could figure at that time. We knew that we would have to adjust our lives to the solar cycle of the new planet.

While the rest of our new family got to work on their projects, I went back to the helm of the ship to contact Luke and check on his project. I also watched more of

Doc's video instructions and listened to the ship's logs to find out if it was the first planet that could support life.

I contacted Luke and Beth to see what they had found.

"Ya, Orian?" Luke said. Luke went on to say, "This planet is beautiful. Beth and I have flown most of the way around the perimeter of the mountains, and the golden color of the mountains is gorgeous. The golden colors of the mountains are actually some sort of plant life, and I took some samples. There are different parts of the mountains that have large, mirror-like rocks. They seem to be gateways to something, but nothing registered on our scanners. I found at least twenty of these mirror-like rocks and one black, mirror-like rock. There are paths from each one that lead to the center of the power source."

Luke also reported that the power source was larger than we ever expected it to be. He could see no logical reason for the source of power or why it even existed. I told Luke and Beth to wrap it up soon and said we would discuss things further when all of us were done for the day.

Shane and the humanoids finished the perimeter force field, which surrounded the living area and planting area and blanketed the ship. This way we could limit the starship's force field and slowly shut down nonessential systems on the ship, giving some of the ship's systems a needed rest.

Doreen and Amanda were doing great work on our outside living quarters, and with the humanoids' help, the main structure was nearly complete.

I realized I could access all the logs and data that Doc had put into the computer from outside the ship with my personal vision gear. I just had to think or speak to the computer, and the vision gear would respond with a virtual screen in front of me that I could access with my hands in midair, moving the icons and opening and closing programs right in front of my face.

I went outside and sat with Doreen. We went through some of the most essential parts of the logs first. One thing we found was that the computer could make anything that we wanted it to. More humanoids, weapons, starships—anything!

"Interesting," Doreen said. "Orian, don't you think we could use some satellites to orbit this new planet? Like the weather satellites on earth? Also to find more land, measure ocean depths, volcanic activity, if there is any?"

"Boy, Doreen, you don't ask for much," I said with a straight face. Then I broke out laughing.

"Way," said Doreen.

"Yes, way," I said.

"Doreen, you ask the computer to create satellites the way you want them and see what happens."

"Got ya, Commander Orian."

She gave me a kiss on the cheek and smiled as she commenced telling the computer what kind of satellites she wanted.

I asked Shane and Amanda to take a stroll around the area and take samples of the plant life and try to communicate with the plant life if they could.

"How are we supposed to talk to a plant with our minds?" Amanda asked.

Shane was laughing and kind of making fun of me. I laughed as well and told them that I really didn't know yet, but all I knew was that we were supposed to be able to if Doc's log was right. So Shane and Amanda went out on their small tour of the area and started to record the plant life and the area surrounding the ship. I could hear Amanda yelling in the distance.

"Hello, plant. Can you hear me? Speak if you can. Can I take a sample of you? I promise it won't hurt you," she yelled and so on.

Doreen and I started laughing so hard that we almost wet our pants.

"I don't think that is the way the mind enhancement is supposed to work. It's for the ability to read minds and communicate with our minds," I told Doreen, but it was funny to hear them try.

Shane and Amanda checked out every little detail of the plant life that they had found so far. Just looking out from the shell of our new house, we could see that the plant life was dense. Some mushroom-like plants that were the size of tall oak trees had tentacles like a squid's that dangled down and reached all the way to the ground from all around the top. Berry-like protrusions popped out all around the tentacles.

Shane and Amanda found tree-like plants that were soft in texture and build and looked more like ferns back on Earth, but they were just huge. Some plants that looked like forty-foot grasses were more like bamboo but with furry, dark green stalks and light purple tips. Others looked like ordinary flowers, some with the sweetest smells like no other plant on Earth. Some were large, orange, lily-shaped flowers, and some looked like daisies but were a dark red with purple ends and a black stem.

Amanda found one plant that had yellow fruit like a banana but in the shape of a watermelon. Amanda took a sample, but first she yelled out "Oh dear plant, can I pick one of your fruit?" Shane was on his knees laughing hard as Amanda talked to the plants, but this was not unusual for Amanda. She always talked to her flower garden and plants on earth. She was still amusing. The fruit was heavy, and they didn't have a humanoid with them so they were limited on what they could carry back to the house.

Shane called me and asked if I could send out a humanoid with a hovercraft to help them with their collections.

"Sure," I told Shane, "but you might want to turn off your mic so Doreen and I can't hear Amanda talking to the plants."

"Cute!" Amanda said, "I heard that! And Orian Grant, what is so funny? You told me to talk to the plant life and ask them to take samples."

"Just kidding," I told her.

"Ya," Doreen told her. "Keep doing what you are doing, Amanda. We are getting a good laugh here."

I told Shane that I would send a hovercraft with a humanoid right away and that he would hone in on Shane's signal.

"Thanks Orian," Shane said.

"Computer," I asked, "will you send a hovercraft to Shane and Amanda and wake up humanoid number twenty-one to help them."

"Yes, Orian." the computer answered.

Soon a beautiful hovercraft came out of the bay. It had the look of a Humvee, but it was as quiet as a hair dryer as it hovered a few inches off the ground. The craft was named Vern. It took off, along with a humanoid, in the search of Amanda and Shane.

Doreen and I went back to check up on the computer logs and had a lot of questions. The main one we had was how to use mind communication.

"How we are supposed to communicate with aliens or any intelligent plant life with our minds?" we asked the computer.

"Orian, look on your security belt," the computer said. "You see that small pouch on the right side?"

"Yes," I said.

"In the pouch you will see a small earpiece," the computer said. "Put that into your ear and that will tie all your neurons together to make telepathic communication possible. You can turn off the human mind communication by just thinking it. After all, you don't want Doreen to know how much you like her, do you, Orian?"

"Yes I do," Doreen said.

I smiled. "Thanks, Computer." I said. Our Doc had made the computers and humanoids have senses of compassion and humor; I sure did miss him.

"Orian," the computer said.

"Yes, Computer," I said.

"Now that you and Doreen are alone together, your father wanted you to listen and see more about the Earth's destruction and the sounds of the people."

"No," I yelled.

"Maybe some other day," the computer said. "Your father wanted you to listen and see all of the pain that he saved you from. But you don't have to watch it all now. And if it bothers you two so much, we can postpone it."

"Yes, I will postpone it for now. Maybe some other time," I said. I was not ready for that yet. It was just too soon.

I turned on Doc's video to the part about things that he had done for us.

"Father," I asked, "in the future, how will we know that we are ready to have children? What should we tell them about our Earth and where we came from?"

"Don't worry, Orian. I have every movie ever made in the library, every book ever made, and the entire internet in your database so you can show your children and your grandchildren and on and on all about Earth and the wonderful place that you grew up in."

"Great," Doreen said. "Thanks, Dr. Grant."

"Even though father is gone, it is nice to be able to talk to him through our computer system."

"Orian," Luke called in then.

"Yes, Luke, what is it? How are you and Beth coming along?"

"Fine, we are at the power source and have put sensors around, but something's strange, Orian. Rivers flowing from the valleys all seem to drain into the center of this large crystal-like object. But as the water flows in, it doesn't come back out. I sent a small probe down into the river and down the well as I call it. The probe went down into the source, so we will see if the probe can pick up any information that we can check on later."

"Good luck," I said.

Luke went on to tell me that he had put sensors on each side of the mirrors all around the range of the mountains. He said that they weren't really mirrors but plasma-like material. They were strong but soft to touch. The computer told me that the strange plasma-like projections might be gateways of sorts.

"We will have to find out more, Luke. Maybe we all will go out on a survey tomorrow. Why don't you and Beth wrap it up soon, and we will all talk over dinner about what we have found out on this new Earth."

"Will do," Luke said in a smart-sounding voice. I told Luke that Shane and Amanda were still out, checking out the surrounding areas and would be a couple of hours.

"Okay," Luke said. "See you soon, Orian."

Soon, Luke and Beth came soaring in. They landed in a shuttle bay. Then Amanda and Shane came back with the samples that they had taken during the day. I told them all to put everything into the science lab and let the computer and the humanoids check out the day's catch. We all sat around our makeshift table in the house and talked about the long day's events.

I was really interested in the mirrors or plasma fields around the mountains and some of the readings of the power source that Luke and Beth found.

Luke told us all that this was a beautiful world. He even saw fish-like creatures in the ocean as he went over one mountaintop and skimmed the waters nearby. Luke said that one fish or animal in the shallows of the shoreline was a massive fish with several fins. It jumped at the ship as it had come in for a closer view.

"That was a close one," Luke said. He told us that he had mistakenly turned off the force field on a stop at one of the plasma fields. "I thought it was going to get us," Luke said. "But Beth turned on the force field just as the fish was taking another lunge at us. I told Beth, 'Well, at least one of us was thinking.' I was laughing inside, but I knew that it could have been a lot worse."

Luke couldn't tell me more about the power source in the center of our new land until the probes sent back more data, but we watched the video of Luke and Beth's adventure around the landmass. We saw that the closer they got to the mountains the denser the plant life was. There were waterfalls all around the mountains, but they did not know where the water was coming from.

"So much to learn here," I said, "but we have plenty of time to get to the heart of this new planet."

Luke did mention that all of the mountainsides were covered with plant life except the plasma-like mirrors.

"Interesting," Amanda said. "Could you see why, Luke?"

"No," Luke said. "Like I said, it was a soft material yet with a moist-to-the-touch feeling."

"Well, let's hope the sensors that you left out will tell us something," I said, "and finally we might find out what these plasma-like objects are."

"I did bring home a small sample of some excess plasma that I found on the ground," Luke said.

"Take the sample to the science room and have the computer analyze it and see how strong it is and if we can use if for anything useful."

"Okay," said Luke.

Luke took the sample down to the science bay along with the plant life and put it in the computer sampling port.

"Luke," the computer said. "This is indeed plasma-like matter but very strong. I can't tell the complete makeup of the sample. Let's see how strong it is."

Luke agreed and had the computer put pressure on the plasma.

"No luck."

The computer fired a phaser beam at it, and still there was no penetration.

"Keep working on it, Computer, and I will join the others," Luke said.

Then out of nowhere the sky darkened. It started to cloud up and get dark really fast. Because there was no roof on top of our new home yet, I yelled, "Back to the ship before we get wet!"

Once there, we watched as the powerful storm approached. The sky turned red. Lighting was striking all over the land. Strange noises came from outside the ship and sounded almost like ghosts. Then there was loud thunder, and rain came down in large, dark blue droplets, drenching everything.

"Computer, adjust the force field so that we get rain inside the area to give our plants in our living area a drink," I said.

"Done, Orian," said the computer.

The winds were strong, and the plants outside, especially the ones shaped like mushrooms, turned upside down on top to create a cone and capture all the rain they could get.

"That would make for a good swimming pool after the rain stops," Doreen said.

It was very dark out. The weird-colored clouds were all red, orange, and yellow—changing all the time as the storm went on. The plants seemed to come to life and turned on the beautiful colors that were imbedded in the plant vines, the roots, and the stalks.

Since the days were so long, I asked the family if we should hit the sack and get a start on the rest of our projects the next day. We all agreed, went to our rooms, and opened the viewers. At least, I fell fast asleep, dreaming of how we were going to cope, rebuild, and repopulate on this new Earth, which we called New Earth Two or planet NE-2.

I was fast asleep when, all of a sudden, the alarms went off. The storm was still raging, and I asked the computer what was wrong.

"Orian, the sensors have detected alien life approaching fast."

I got dressed in a hurry and even put my shoes on the wrong feet and tripped. *Fool*, I thought to myself.

"Computer, turn on all force fields outside!"

"Already done, Orian." the computer said.

Luke, Shane, and the girls were all coming into the bridge area when I asked the computer to open the viewer. All around the ship, the sky was full of lighting, but this time, strange-looking creatures flew about the ship. Some landed outside the defenses, trying to test us. They seemed curious as to who we were and where we had come from.

"Where, Computer, did these bugs or whatever they are come from?"

"From one of the plasma fields," the computer said. "And also sensors placed at the power source detected them."

"Luke," I said, "you and Beth stay with the ship. Doreen, you and Shane, Amanda, and I will take one of the ships out and try to communicate with these creatures."

"We will get ready," Doreen said.

I told Shane and Amanda not to forget to put on their safety belts, and I told them about the mind-reading device in their belts.

"Okay," everyone said.

"And we all will be ready in five minutes," Shane said.

Once we were all ready, we went to the shuttle bay, and I told Shane to sit up front with me and Doreen and Amanda to sit behind us. I told everyone to put in their earpieces. Once the earpieces were in our heads, they were full of strange words. Then the translations started to come through. As we lifted off and went outside, we flew among the creatures, and they seemed to want to attack the ship.

"What do you want?" was going through our heads. We heard, "Should we try to destroy them?" We were trying to get used to the mind reading and figure out how to answer them, but we had to get used to thinking their way to be able to answer them.

"Where did you come from?" we heard as a six-winged, dragonfly went flying by. It had two feet hanging beneath its wings and hands that looked like a smashed potato with eight fingers; it was just strange looking. I landed by the power source and stopped the ship. What seemed to be the leader of this six-winged creature came toward us. It was thrown back by the force field.

Then I tried the mind communication earpiece to see if I could communicate with them. I thought, *We mean you no harm*, but there was no reply.

"Computer, am I using the mind device the right way? I can hear them all over the place, but they can't hear me!"

"You have to talk back to them," the computer said, "and then it will be transferred to their minds."

"Okay," I said to the computer. "Did you hear that, Doreen?"

"Yes," she said.

"Let's all talk to them, but let me talk to the leader first," I said. "Hello, my name is Orian, and we mean you no harm."

The dragonfly creature asked, "Who are you and what world did you come from?"

"We left our planet many, many, light-years away before it was destroyed by our sun," I said. "We landed here because it can support our human life-form.

Shane then asked the creature, "What is your species' name?"

The dragonfly creature said, "We are called Leamarkes." The Leamarke went on to say "How do we know that you are a friendly alien, and what world did you appear from?"

"I said that our world, called Earth, was destroyed, and we came here in a starship," I said.

"Is that what that is?"

"Yes," Doreen said.

"How many of you are there?" the Leamarke asked.

"Just six of us," Doreen said.

I asked the Leamarke if it and some of its friends would like to come and discuss things in our shuttle bay.

"How do we know it is not a trap?" the Leamarke asked.

"No trap," I said. "I have so many questions to ask about where you come from."

Finally, the Leamarke said, "By the way, my name is Satar."

"My name is Orian," I said. "With me is my brother Shane, my girlfriend Doreen, and Amanda. Follow our ship to our starship, and we will talk, and you can tell us what your world is like and why are you flying in this storm."

"That is easy," Satar said. "This is a safe time to go to the source and gather our offerings. Most of the aliens in the other worlds don't like stormy weather."

"What other worlds?" I asked.

Lightning hit our force field with the strength of one of our crystal cannons and shorted out some of our instruments.

"Computer, will you increase the force field to one hundred percent?" I asked. "Just to be on the safe side. Please do it, even if we need more power."

"If I can do that with the damage." the computer said.

Our ship headed toward the ground until, all of a sudden, the backup systems turned on and we stabilized.

"Wow, that was a close one," Amanda said.

"Sure was," Shane replied. "Hope the ship is fine. What kind of power can be such a strong force against our defenses?"

"Satar, are you still there?" I yelled.

"Yes," Satar said.

"Then follow us to our ship so we can talk."

Satar and a group of five others came. Out of thousands of Leamarkes, only five were chosen to join him.

"Computer, track the Leamarkes and let them through the force field into the shuttle bay," I said.

"Okay, Orian, but be careful. You can't trust anything yet."

"Okay," I told the computer.

Soon the careful Leamarkes followed us into the shuttle bay and landed on the shuttle bay floor. As we landed, the humanoids started to repair the ship.

Luke and Beth greeted us there with their weapons drawn, just in case.

"Luke, Beth," I said, "this is Satar. He is a Leamarke. Luke, put in your earpiece to understand them and join in."

"Okay," Luke and Beth said.

I asked the computer which sensor had gone off first.

"On the plasma field fourteen miles away," the computer said.

"That was plasma field number five," Luke said. "I went around the mountain in a clockwise motion."

"Satar," I said, "you and your friends make yourselves comfortable."

"Luke, did the ship get hit by lighting from this storm?"

"Yes," Luke said, "but with little damage, and it has already been fixed."

"Good, Luke, we had a close one."

With the shuttle bay doors open, we could hear the storm rage on and the rain pound on the ground. We were scared by everything, and now with Leamarkes on the ship, we were wondering "How is this going to play out?"

"What is this thing we are on, and how do you live here?" Satar asked.

"This is our shuttle bay where we keep our spacecraft and flying travel machines. We live on a different level of this craft," I said.

"I see," said Satar.

His friends keep on talking about a trap. They were not talking but just thinking, which I could still hear.

"Satar, would you and your friends like something to eat or drink?"

"Sure," said Satar and some of his friends or guards.

"Tell the computer what you want and how it is made so we can create your food and drink."

"What is a computer?" Satar asked.

"A very smart being that makes our lives easier and helps us communicate with you and others we might meet," I said. "Satar, what did you mean by worlds or planets? And how did you get here?"

"Have you noticed any shiny spaces in the mountains around you?" Satar asked.

"Yes," I said.

"Well, in my world, there is only one sun and a whole different solar system."

"How come we can't get into your world or continent," Luke asked in amazement and with a serious face. "We can't even blast a hole in it to get in if that is a portal."

"Yes," Satar said. "You have to have a code and permission to enter."

"Go on," I said to Satar.

"Well, Satar said, "we can see out through our portals, but the outsiders can't see in. We saw the strange flying craft go by our portal and put some shiny objects by the edge of our portal. We have guards at the portal to protect us and warn us of any breach or an invasion."

"What is your world like, Satar?" Doreen asked.

"Unlike this world. We don't know how we got there or where we are compared to your world that you chose to call your new home."

"We believe in evolution and that we have existed for years, but we have nothing like what you have here to visit the stars. Is there more intelligent life like yours on your planet, and what is your planet called?"

"Planet Tuare is the name of our world," Satar said. Satar went on to tell us that planet Tuare has only one sun called Luminous. Tuare has two moons and has many stars in its skies.

"Satar," I asked, "are you the only species in your world? Does it have plant life like ours?"

"No plant life likes yours, but we do have different tribes that share our planet. One group is called Darps; others we just consider animals, except for the Raters. We are at war with them and try to leave them alone, but they have raided our homes on different occasions, and we have to be ready to attack at any time."

"Satar," Amanda said, "We call them wars on our planet, and it just seems like people of our species never get along; we always had war on our former planet."

"Interesting," Satar said. "Can everyone, on your destroyed planet, have had things like you have here to fight wars?"

"No," Amanda said, "this is a much intended invention that Orian's father, Doc, created and has many defenses that the people on Earth never had."

"You mention weapons, Satar. Can I see your weapon please?" I asked.

"Sure," said Satar. He asked one of his friends, named Zanter, to show us their weapons.

"What should I shoot at?" Zanter asked.

"Hold on," I said. "I will put up a piece of leftover material from the shuttle bay. Shoot that, Zanter."

Zanter looked at the piece of composite material and ejected a flame ball of spit out of his mouth at the material. He hit it dead on but did no damage.

"Well," Zanter said, "I guess our weapons do not work in this world."

Then we went to our phaser and took a shot, and blue the composite material blew all the way across the room just on fire.

"I never saw anything like that," said Satar.

I asked a humanoid to gather some of the leftover material and have the computer scan it. Then another humanoid came in with weird-looking plant life with bug-like things in it and a dark blue drink for the Leamarkes.

"How did you know what food that we like to eat?" asked Satar.

"Well, our computer can read your minds and create anything that you ask it to."

"Amazing," said Satar. "But how do you speak our language?"

"Through our earpieces in our ears; they help us communicate with anything that has a thought process. We have to move our mouths and talk for you to understand us," I said.

We all talked to the Leamarke people and told them a little about us. Slowly, we gained their trust.

It was still raining and thundering loudly, and lightning kept hitting the ship. But with the force field expanded to 100 percent, the ship stood firm. Satar said that, when the storm started to lessen, they would have to leave for home to avoid things that came out of different worlds.

"What worlds?" I asked Satar again.

"See," Satar said, "other times that we have been out, we have seen different aliens come out of other plasma fields, and we have had some confrontations with them."

"When the weather clears," I said, "we will give you and all your kind a safe trip back to your world."

We all looked out of the shuttle bay into the storm. Thousands of Leamarkes were flying and standing just outside the force field. Orange eyes stared at us, looking with wonderment. Then several mosquito-like things were flying around the Leamarkes. They had long stingers and were trying to suck blood out of the Leamarkes. I saw fireballs shoot at the mosquitoes, and then they disappeared.

"They are a nuisance," Satar said.

"From your world?"

"Yes," Satar said with a sigh.

I asked Satar how we could visit his world and see what his world was like.

"Not safe for you yet," Satar said. "We will have to take a vote first with the rest of my tribe and see what they say. With your weapons, you could betray our trust and destroy our world and all the Leamarkes."

I told Satar that I wanted him to come over again tomorrow so we could talk further. "And I can show you our ship's video logs, and you can see more of what we are like and what we have left behind."

"Fine," Satar said. He was getting ready to leave when I stopped him and asked him to wait one minute.

"Computer, send down humanoid number twenty-six, and I will send it back with Satar with information on us and to show them some hologram videos of our history and our ship and what we can offer."

"What is a humanoid?" Satar asked.

"Remember that human-looking man who brought you your food?"

"Yes," Satar said.

"Well, he was created by our computer and made in the likeness of us. Can he go with you? You can communicate with him and learn about us and our journey and our plans. He will be armed just in case you get in trouble with the Raters on the way to your homes. Please take this as a gesture of our newfound trust in your people. Then if you want, you can come here tomorrow while we are working on our outside housing and more exploration. You can contact us through number twenty-six and let us know that you are coming."

Satar looked unwilling at first, but then he agreed to take the humanoid.

As we were waiting for the humanoid, a bolt of lightning hit the force field, and the whole place shook.

"Computer" I said, "what is the force behind these strong lightning strikes? Wasn't this ship designed to blast through a planet at lightspeed and not get damaged?"

"Yes. This lightning is more like a weapon in grade," the computer said. "I will try to capture some of its energy. Maybe we can make another weapon with this intense power."

Bam—another hit.

"Computer, how many more can we take until force field breakdown?"

"The field will hold, Orian. And I have harnessed some of the energy with the last hit."

Bam. It was a stronger hit, and there was more shaking. We were starting to panic, but the Leamarkes said that the lighting had never hit one of them. They were surprised by its power.

"Yes, but nothing has penetrated the force field this much before," I told them. "Satar, here comes the humanoid. Let me give it some instructions quickly." I told the humanoid to be careful and to take air samples, measure gravity intensity, and get more information on the culture. "And find out how to get in when you go through the portal. Twenty-six, keep your force field on high and, if attacked, return fire." I turned to Satar. "There you go, Satar. He is all yours. Have fun, and please join us tomorrow. We can discuss your world more, and maybe you will trust us more. Thanks for the nice meeting with both you and your friends."

Then off went Satar, and we watched his people as they flew back to the portal. They stood guard until our humanoid arrived.

Days went by as we waited for either our humanoid or for Satar to return so we could visit the Leamarkes' home. In the meantime, we worked to complete the living quarters outside. We got it ready to withstand a strong storm like we had had a few days before. Doreen was busy bossing the humanoids around, telling them how she wanted the house built and where to put things. The computer was busy making cupboards and other things that you would see in a house.

I told Doreen that she was doing fine and that I wanted to check on Luke and Shane and see if they wanted to go fishing to see what kind of life lived in NE-2's oceans.

"Shane, Luke, you want to try fishing?" I asked when I found them.

"Sure, but with what, Orian? We don't have fishing poles, and we don't know what these ocean creatures like to eat."

"Well, you guys, we will make this a science trip along with fishing to catch one of these fish and see if they are good to eat. We'll also check what seaweeds have as vitamins and if they are edible."

"Let's go," Luke said.

"And get the shuttle ready, so we can go now."

"Right on," Luke said.

We all got into the shuttle and headed out toward the sea.

"Over there," Luke said. "That is where I almost got ate by that creature. Be careful, Orian."

"Aaahh, don't worry, Luke, I got this."

All of a sudden, a large fish that looked like the Loch Ness monster jumped up and tried to grab us. I hit the joystick forward and took off like a quick wind.

"Well, I guess the fish here like us for food," Shane said.

We all laughed, and I said, "We will take another pass, and if he jumps again, we will hit him with a phaser on stun."

"You're the boss," Shane said.

"You're nuts," Luke said.

"This force field can take any hit," I said with a lot of confidence.

I turned the ship around and went back to the area where we had gotten attacked. I flew closer to the water, just skimming the surface.

"You're looking for trouble," Luke said.

"Don't worry, guys, I got this," I said.

Then behind us, a large duck-billed, three-humped animal jumped up and swallowed us.

"Way to go, Orian," Luke said. "What do we do now?"

The onboard computer said the force field's stability was falling down to 65 percent.

"What is going on?" I asked the computer.

"The acid in this animal's stomach is penetrating the field, and I can't compensate."

"What do we do now?" Shane screamed.

We turned upside down and sideways. I tried to hold onto the controls to go to lightspeed to shoot through the animal, but I couldn't reach it.

"Field down to forty percent," the computer blasted out.

"Shane, hit the phaser button if you can reach it."

"I can't," Shane said.

We were completely upside down and going deeper into the sea. The pressure gauge in the ship was blinking red.

"Fields at twenty percent," said the computer.

"Computer, can you take control and get us out of here?"

"No," the computer said, "this force field should take anything that you can throw at it."

Then the creature started upward, and we got thrown backward in the ship.

"Now no one is at the helm," I yelled. "Luke, you are the small one. Can you climb over us and hit the lightspeed button?"

"Can't do that," Luke said. "We might head into the crust of this planet and be destroyed."

Off went the lights, and we were in complete darkness.

"Come on, guys," I said. "We are going to die if we don't do something—and quick!"

Finally, Luke got over his piled-up brothers and humanoids. He tried to hit the phaser switch.

"Can't do it," Luke screamed.

"Ten percent force field," the computer said.

"Humanoid, can you hit the phaser or plasma gun to get us out of here?"

"I will try to force my way to the helm," Number seven said.

Then around in circles we went inside the belly of the beast; by now we were all bruised up and shaken.

"My arm is broken," Shane yelled in agony. "Please help me." Amanda looked at Shane's arm, and things didn't look good. Luke was the strong one; he was making me look bad.

"Hurry up, Seven," he yelled, "and blast us out of here."

"We don't have much power left in the lazerpon torpedo bay."

Then I heard number seven say, "Almost there."

Then finally Seven was able to hit the plasma lazerpon torpedo's button, and—*boom*—flesh and parts of the great big fish went all over the ocean. Soon we were deep down under moving toward the ocean floor. We kept sinking deep down into the darkness.

"Four thousand feet down," I yelled. "We are still sinking. Luke, help me figure a way to get out of this mess!"

We all thought that we were going to die.

"Shields at five percent and declining," I said.

"Luke, get us back to the starship!"

"Give me a few minutes," Luke said. "I have to wait until we stabilize at this depth."

"The shields are still declining," I yelled.

"The shields are at one percent," Luke yelled as we started upward toward the surface.

"Some hull damage as well," I said. "And at these depths, I don't know if we can last much longer. Computer," I asked "can you get us back online?"

"Working on it," the computer said.

The humanoid was working to fix the components inside the ship that had gotten damaged.

"Six thousand feet. Seven thousand feet," the computer said. "The hull will breach in two minutes."

Then all of a sudden, the backup lights and power came back on, and we were back in action. Luke was the first one at the helm and got control of the ship as we were sinking again.

I took over the helm, and Luke was at my side. I told him how brave he was and that I was sorry for freaking out.

"That's okay, brother, but this planet is not like anything that we have encountered before," Luke said. "The starship and our force fields are not working as well as expected. We will have to ask the computer to see if we can configure a different force field for this planet."

"I agree, Luke."

I pointed the shuttle upward, and up we went to the surface.

"Get in the air," Shane screamed. "I don't want to go through that again."

"Thank god," I said. "That was a close one and closer than I ever want to get to death again."

"I agree," Shane said. He was moaning in pain. "Please get me back to the ship." Shane yelled in pain as his arm dangled downward.

Up we went, and as we looked down, the sea was full of green blood and small fish that were eating the floating flesh.

"Now that is the kind of fish we should catch. We might have to kill a big fish or animal and then net the smaller fish after."

"Could be, but sounds like extreme fishing to me," Luke said.

We took off, limping back toward our starship as the acid kept eating at the hull of our shuttle. We thought we might crash before we got to the shuttle bay. The ship was making noises, and sparks were flying all over the place.

"I hope that we make it over the mountains. Up," I said. I pulled back on the joystick. The ship rose upward, but the mountains were dead ahead.

"Are we going to crash?" Shane asked in a painful voice.

"I think we're going to make it," I answered.

The mountains got closer and closer as I tried to gain altitude—no luck.

"Hold on," I yelled as I banked toward the left, just missing the mountains by a few feet. "I will have to head toward the valleys in order to get us home. Luke, can you work on the ship's propulsion system and get us more power?"

"I will try," Luke replied.

The ship was failing fast, so I said to the computer, "Can you help us with this problem?"

"Orian," the computer answered, "land the ship if you can in the cargo bay. I will have the humanoids put a special material down so you can land on it. I don't want the acid to touch the starship at all."

On our way off to find the valley, we were hovering just off the ground, and I yelled to Shane, "Shields at zero percent." Then I asked in a shaky and raspy voice, "Computer, will the hull hold until we get to the bay?"

"It should, Orian," the computer replied.

"There's the valley," Luke yelled. "I see it."

I banked to the right down the valley's throat. As I headed toward our destination, we clipped the bamboo-like trees, crashed through the mushroom-like plant life, and skimmed through the fern-like trees. *Bash, boom.* The shipped rocked as we hit every object that was in our way with no shield to protect us.

Then I saw the starship in the distance and tried to keep our height and speed steady to get us home.

"Look," Amanda said. "The hull has a hole in it, and the acid is dripping down."

"Don't touch it, Amanda, or any one of you."

"You don't have to worry about that, Orian. Will she hold?" Shane asked.

"I think we can make it," I replied. "Hold on this is going to be a rough landing!" We approached the cargo bay. "Computer, will the material stop the acid from eating through the landing site?"

"I have created a material after I analyzed the acid on your ship, and it should stop any breach."

Finally, we got into the cargo bay, and I tried to land on the landing site which was all lit up.

"Hold on," I said to everyone, "here we go."

Then with a large bounce and a backbreaking and quick stop, we landed.

Doreen and Beth greeted us at the ship and asked, "What happened to the ship, and are you guys okay?"

"No," said Luke. "Shane has a broken arm. Can you take him to the infirmary?"

"Yes," said Amanda, "Come with me."

A humanoid helped Shane get off the ship and got him ready for the infirmary.

"Don't touch anything that looks like acid when you get off the ship," I said.

I opened the ship's door, and the team of humanoids was waiting to take care of Shane when he got off the ship. To my amazement, there was a team of humanoids that looked like doctors and nurses. They took Shane to the infirmary.

Meanwhile, back in the shuttle bay, I told Luke to help me shut down the ship's systems; even the core of the main reactor had to be shut down. Acid hit my arm, but fortunately, the material of my suit saved me from the acid. Luke and I shut down the systems of the shuttle and hurriedly got off the ship.

When we were all out of the ship, I looked at it. I couldn't believe all the damage, as the acid kept eating away at the shuttle.

"What is this stuff?" I asked.

"An unknown substance," the computer said. It went on to say that it would work on a way to compensate the shields to be able to handle that kind of acid and even make the ship stronger. "This ship is a complete loss" the computer said.

"I agree, Computer. Now what?"

The computer told me that it would build another shuttle that would be able to take any kind of damage and reflect the acid.

"Orian, go to the helm of the starship and turn on the log that contains the name 'Battles that we have encountered.'"

At the helm, I searched the computer's log and found the file. I started to watch it on the viewer and saw that the starship had had many battles.

"Come here, everyone," I said over the loudspeakers.

When we had all gathered at the viewer—Doreen standing there with her beautiful smile; Amanda still shaken up from the experience; Luke with a curious look; Beth looking exciting and curious; and Shane with a metal splint that had lights on it on his arm—I asked Shane if he was in pain.

"No, I feel fine and can use this arm already," Shane said. "That infirmary is outstanding."

"Watch this, you guys," I said. I started the log, and it was just like watching a movie. We watched as the voice on the log file showed us the planets that we had landed on for supplies and one of our 250 billion trips. On one planet that looked like a square chess table and that had an earth-like atmosphere, strange-looking creatures with powerful weapons shot at Doc and at the starship's defenses. As the ship got its ore for Doc's inventions, the ship took on damage, and the ship's robots were continually working on the ship for repairs. We noticed that Doc was returning fire. As the ship took off, its lazerpon torpedoes fired on the bases and did a lot of damage to the enemy as well. Ships took off in pursuit of our ship and fired phaser-like beams at us. The ship's force field was failing, but it held as we fired back and destroyed most of the ships that were firing on us. Then Doc put us into lightspeed, and the threat was gone.

The log went on to show that we had stopped at other planets. We were intercepted by starships that hailed us. With his mind communication earpiece, Doc heard the voices saying to hold on and be ready to be boarded, but Doc told them that we were a science ship from a lost planet, just looking for a place to live.

"Not here," a fat frog crossed with a lizard said. "Leave or you will be destroyed."

"Not until we get some supplies from your planet," Doc said. Then the ships fired upon us, and the ship jolted.

"All power to the force fields," Doc said. He fired back. *Bam*—the lazerpon torpedoes hit the enemy's ship and exploded. The ship slowly burned and fell toward the planet.

"Hail the ship," Doc said with a humanoid at his side at the helm. "You are no match for us," Doc told the fat lizard. "Either you let us land and get ore for our ship or we will destroy your ship."

"Very well," the lizard-like creature said. "You won, but hurry, and don't plan on trying to stay on our world."

"Okay," Doc said.

Then the ore ships went to the surface and gathered material and brought back more than five thousand tons of ore and materials and put the ore in a bay that we hadn't even seen yet.

"This is great! It's so exciting," Doreen said.

We watched as our ship flew from star system to star system. On one planet, Doc found life, but the atmosphere was more of a sulfur compound with carbon dioxide—not suitable for humans, but the large brainless creatures were docile in nature.

We watched for what seemed like hours. We got into several fire fights in the journey, and the force field held.

"Okay, Computer, enough for now," I said. "Get busy trying to make our force fields adapt to this planet. And can you make our force field belt able to compensate for different situations that we might encounter on this new planet? And new worlds that we might explore."

"Orian, I have already captured the force of the lighting that hit us and copied its power and put it into your weapons. Just say 'lighting mode' and your weapons will do as you command," the computer said.

Chapter Four

Doreen had our new living quarters just about finished, and Beth was designing the kitchen and bedrooms. I told Doreen that she had designed a beautiful home.

"Look, Doreen," I said, "you even got the humanoids to put in the garden and fences for the cattle and other animals."

"I am glad that I was not with you guys after what you went through," she said. Doreen went on to tell me that the computer had said that the water from the river was safe to drink and that we even had running water in our new house.

"Great," I said. "I could use some water." I took a drink of the water, and it tasted great. It was nice and cold, though a little sweet.

Beth told us that the soil was very rich in minerals, including some not known by us on Earth, but they were safe to plant in. So Beth said that we would have a nice garden now, and soon we would be able to eat nice fresh, grown food again.

I was worried about the humanoid that I had sent with Satar into his world. He hadn't returned yet. The computer reminded me that days were different on that world than on Earth and that, really, he had only been gone one day according to NE-2's orbit and revolution.

I was taking a walk into the new land alone with a humanoid called Mark. He was different from the other humanoids. He was dressed in a different style than the others. Mark had a uniform on like the ones we wore, and he could talk with more emotion than the rest. Somehow, he reminded me of my father; he was always in the science room inventing things—weird. But he made a good companion.

We strolled deep into the wilderness and found the path that led to where Satar's world was. I walked in a place where the vines reached out to touch me, and some of the plants tried to eat me. At least, that's what I thought.

After I walked down the path, I came to the plasma gateway. Out of the plasma gateway came Satar and the humanoid.

"Hi, Satar," I yelled, "I was just thinking of you, thinking to myself, and talking to this funny-looking creature."

"And yes," Satar said, "you and your friends may enter."

The humanoid said, "Orian, this is a nice world, but it has a lot of turmoil in it. We got attacked within minutes of our arrival. We will have to try to make peace here."

"Satar, are you hungry?"

"I'm starving," Satar said.

"Well, then, gather some of your friends, and we will have a nice meal in our new home."

"Orian, you and your humanoid come with me, and we will gather my friends. We will go to our tribe area."

"Fine," I said.

Then into the new world we went. I saw a whole new place—new plant life, new bright sun and the world was hotter than the one I had just left. It had a large moon that stood out next to the sun. It seemed like we could reach out and touch it.

"Satar, where is your home or tribe?"

"Just over there, Orian. Can you fly?" Satar asked.

"Fly? No, I can't."

"Well, we live up there," he said.

I looked up, and there was a landmass floating in the air with falls raining down on us.

"How are we going to get up there, Satar, and how does the light flow through your land and not leave a shadow?"

"That is just the way it is," Satar said.

The next thing I knew was Satar letting out a yell. Down from the floating land came this large land bridge that we could walk up.

"Hurry," Satar said. "The Anomies might follow us and attack us. The Anomies are enemies from years ago, and we have fought over the bottom land for planting rights and food forever. This world is scarce in food resources for our large population."

I was halfway up the walkway when a large rhino-looking animal with a hammerhead shark's head started slamming trees down and coming right for us.

"Hurry," Satar said, so we ran the rest of the way up. Satar spit a blast of fire toward the beast, and it turned away. Once we were on the floating island of Satar's, I was greeted by several Leamarkes, and I felt at home.

"Orian?" Mark asked. "See, this is what I meant, that the worlds of the universe may have many surprises."

"Boy, Mark, you sound like my father," I said and laughed.

The Leamarkes talked about the war with the anomies and about how the Anomies used the Leamarkes as a food source. *Terrible*, I thought.

"Can we help?" I asked.

"Maybe," Satar said. "With your technology, we can defeat them."

"Well, Satar, if we give you weapons, that will only start more wars. That is what happened on our planet many years ago."

"Then how can we beat the anomies?" Satar asked.

"I will go and talk to them at some time, but first, I and the others will fight on your side until an agreement can be made."

"Whatever you do, don't go by the edge of the land. You can get killed from there."

I went to the edge of the floating landmass and looked over the edge. All I saw were some animals that looked like dog-and-cat mixtures running in packs. Large trees reached into the sky and shaded the Leamarkes land.

The floating landmass had flowing water and its own types of plant life, though it was more of a wild flower–type landmass than one with trees. I didn't know what kept the landmass floating, but I wouldn't question creation. I saw large trees that seemed to go forever up into the sky, and down from those trees came large vines that seemed to be attached to the landmass, keeping it afloat. I noticed that the landmass we were on was made of a woven material that would actually let the sunlight get down to the plants below it so the plants could survive.

"Satar, this is an amazing place. How large is this world?" I asked.

"This plane goes on for many miles," Satar said. "Beyond our land, it seems that the rest of our world is desert." Satar also said that there was a strange but powerful group of creatures that lived in a vast desert. "We call them Trites. I will tell you more about them when we meet again."

"Satar," I said, "why are you and Anomies fighting?"

I looked down from the landmass and saw the Anomies gathering around the base of the landmass.

"We are ready to fight," Satar said. I told him that I would help but that I first wanted to talk to the Anomies to try to communicate with them. Anomies were furry little creatures. They looked something like our teddy bears we had back on earth.

"Satar," I said, "they don't look that mean to me."

With my mind communication earpiece, I could hear the Anomies yelling to the Leamarkes, "We will destroy your world, and then we will be the ones to have control of the water source."

"Satar, lower the land bridge. I want to see what the Anomies have to say."

"Orian," Satar said, "if I lower the bridge, the Anomies will come up and try to destroy us."

There was one Anomie that was kind of a brown color with eyes the size of baseballs. They all had small hands and small feet and had bows and arrows strung over their shoulders, but they don't look that dangerous to me.

I called out to the Anomies. I looked at the one that looked like the leader, and I told him that we were from the other side of the gateway, and we just landed on the planet.

"We are from a planet called Earth that was destroyed by a solar storm. We are friendly people, and we're the only ones left from our home planet. What is your name?" I asked him.

"Tara," he answered.

"My name is Orian, Tara. My humanoid and I would like to come down and talk to you. Will you stop the fighting for today?"

"Come on down," Tara said "and we will talk, but don't bring any Leamarkes with you."

"Satar, will you please lower the land bridge?"

"Yes," Satar said, "But if any Anomies try to come up the land bridge, we will fight."

"We will not come up today," Tara said. "Let your friends come down so we can meet with them. We will fight another day."

I asked Satar how we could open the gateway so we could come and visit. Then Satar gave me a ring that would open and close the gateway.

"Thank you, Satar. We will be back soon. Is it okay if we harvest some of the plant life that you have here that is hard? Our people like to have fires, and we like to cook with wood sometimes to make our meals."

"If you need some of our hardwood plant life," Satar said, "please get it deep in the jungle."

"Thanks, Satar. May I have an extra ring for Luke and Shane so they can come and visit anytime they want? I promise you that I will be able to fly up here next time," I said, and I smiled with a lot of confidence.

As Satar got a ring so we could enter his new world, I asked my favorite humanoid to monitor the gateway as we went through it.

"Mark, do this in private and put it in the computer system. Then we can analyze how to get into these worlds without the use of rings, special codes, or other devices that these people use."

"Yes, sir," Mark said. "That should be an easy task."

"Good," I said. Then Satar came and gave me a very shiny device. He called it a ring, but there was no way that it could be used on our fingers.

"Can we just hold the device and open the gateway?" I asked Satar. "Tara, we'll be down shortly. I just have a few more questions to ask, and then we'll come down to meet you," I called down. Then most of the Anomies dissipated, except for Tara and about twenty other Anomies.

"Satar," I said, "tell me a little bit about these worlds on the other sides of the gateways. Have you been in some of the other gateways, and what is on the other side?"

"Yes, I have," Satar said. "You see, Orian, it wasn't always like this. There used to be war between all of the other worlds through the gateways. Then according to our ancestors, many million years ago, there was a big battle, and we made an agreement that each and every one of us would not interfere with or enter the other gateways again.

"You see, Orian, these battles lasted for thousands and thousands of years and just about destroyed all of our worlds. We finally came to a peace agreement when we found ways to use our own resources and to be able to live within our own world without having to fight other worlds for precious resources. There were women without husbands, children without fathers or families— oh, Orian, it was a bad time."

"Satar, lower your bridge so I can go to talk to Tara."

"Okay, Orian." Satar yelled, "Lower the bridge."

I told Satar to stop by anytime with his friends. I told him that there would always be peace between us.

As the bridge lowered, I said good-bye to Satar and asked him if he would try to keep the peace between his people and the Anomies.

"We will try," Satar said.

Once we got to the bottom of the bridge, I walked toward Tara, and he slowly pulled out his bow. He asked me if I had weapons.

"Yes, I do," I said, "to be used on our enemies, which you are not . . . as yet."

Tara and I stared into each other's eyes, trying to decide the best way to ask questions and try to be friendly. I slowly approached Tara and his group and told him that we were not interfering with either the Anomies or the Leamarkes.

"Fine," Tara said. "You are not from our world."

"I agree," I told Tara. "All we want to do is to start a new life on the other side of the gateway." I told Tara that our planet called Earth had been destroyed as we left and had had many fights between different nations, as we called them. "Tara, I want you and your friends to be able to come to our home and enjoy each other's company. But for now, I have to leave and get back to the others."

I gathered my humanoid Mark, and we opened the gateway and left the strange world. I thought while walking back toward our starship. *How can I stop this fighting between the two creatures that I just met, and bring peace to that world?*

"Did you get readings while we walked through the gateway?" I asked Mark.

"Yes," Mark said, "and everything is ready to be put into the mainframe computer." The humanoid went on to say, "If this gateway we just went through is similar to the others, than I think we can open each gateway. But, Orian, while you were talking to Satar and Tara, I scanned the weapons that they have. We have one problem, Orian."

"What is that, Mark?" I asked my humanoid.

"On this planet," Mark said, "things are a lot different than on all the other planets and enemies that our starship has encountered up to this moment. Our force fields held, and we won just about every battle while you were sleeping. I think we will again. I have to put time and input into the mainframe computer on the starship and reconfigure our defenses."

"Fine," I said. "But Mark, first, I want to get home and check on the others."

"Shane, how are you feeling?"

"Fine," Shane said. "The splint seems to be holding, and the bone is healing on its own."

"That is good news, Shane. How long did the doctor humanoids tell you that you have to keep your cast on?" I asked.

"With this new technology that Doc has made for us, my arm will be as good as new by tomorrow," Shane said.

"You're kidding," I said to Shane.

"No, I am not," Shane said.

"Computer," I said, "how could this be?"

"Just remember, Orian," the computer said, "you have been asleep for over two hundred fifty billion years, and with your dad's commands and programming, he gave me the power to create new technologies, such as the humanoids, which your Doc started. And all his advancements over the years we used for the starship. I know that things have changed a lot, Orian, but just remember that this starship and everything in it was all part of your dad's great plan. And, Orian, since you are the oldest, you should understand that Doc gave me emotions and feelings to make you feel more at home with your dad at your side. You will have a surprise someday, Orian. Just keep Mark, your personal humanoid, close to you and listen to him and respect his opinions."

"I will do that," I said. "Thank you, Computer."

As I was talking to the computer, Doreen walked in.

"Orian, why do you look so sad and talk to the computer so much?" she asked.

"Doreen, sometimes talking to the computer and my humanoid Mark is like, somehow, I am talking to my father," I said.

"You really miss your father, don't you, Orian?" Doreen asked.

"You just don't know how much I miss him" I said. "Doreen, there is so much we have to learn on this new planet. How are you coping with the loss of your family? You know, Doreen, we have to be strong for the others, and try to make this our new home. We have been friends all of our lives. Once we get established on our new planet, we will have to think about starting a family." I started blushing as I got ready to tell Doreen that I had loved her all my life. "Doreen, I hope you feel the same way I do. I love you. Will you be my partner for life?"

"I thought you'd never ask, Orian," Doreen yelled. "And yes, I love you too."

Chapter Five

Doreen and the humanoids were putting the final touches on our new home. Beth and Amanda were down in the livestock bay trying to figure out, with help from the computer and some humanoids, how my father planned on getting embryos to grow inside the livestock. The computer told Amanda and Beth to have the humanoids put the embryos in the pens at the end with blue fluid in them and to turn on each device. Then the animals would grow into livestock.

"Great," Amanda said. "Real milk, someday . . . and meat!"

I was studying logs on the computer system while Doreen was outside working on our house with the humanoids. All of a sudden, Satar and his friends appeared at our front gate. Doreen asked the computer to find me and ask the rest of the gang to come down to the house.

I left the logs and started down the long hallway in the starship. I met up with Shane and found Amanda and Beth heading out the door to meet up with Doreen and invite our new friends in. Luke was nowhere to be found. I pressed the intercom button.

"Luke, where are you?" I asked.

"I'm in the shuttle bay fixing the damaged shuttle, and we are almost done," Luke said.

"Luke, stop what you are doing and come down and meet our friends."

"I will be right down," Luke said.

I asked the computer to open the gate so our friends could enter.

"Come on in, Satar," I said. "What a surprise! I was just telling everyone earlier today about your world and some of the problems you have there. Would you like to eat something?"

"Yes," Satar said.

Doreen had made a special table that would accommodate the Leamarkes a lot better when they came for dinner with their large wings and huge bodies. It was a lot easier for Satar and his friends. I asked Satar if he and his friends if they would like to try human food.

"We could try," Satar said.

"Computer," I said, "make us a nice steak dinner with mashed potatoes and gravy and some nice sweet corn."

As we all sat down to eat, I noticed Satar and his friends were bowing as if in prayer. I was amused and asked Doreen to give thanks for the meal. After the giving of thanks, she told all of us how lucky we were to be able to have such wonderful food and to be thankful we were still alive.

As Satar and his friends tried our food, they were amazed by how tasty it was. I told Satar and his friends about how much food we had grown on our planet and how we were lucky to have plenty to eat. I went on to explain that some countries had not had the resources to have bountiful food available to them.

Some of Satar's friends wanted to learn more about our planet. I told them more stories, and then I said, "Amanda, you are a history major. Tell Satar and his friends a little about our planet."

Amanda told Satar and his friends about our oceans and vast continents with all kinds of different people like us. Amanda went on to tell Satar and his friends about all different kinds of animals that we had had our planet and about how some of our animals were kind and loving while other animals were very wild. Amanda went on for hours, telling Satar and his friends about the history of our planet.

At the end of our long talk, I told Satar that we had to retire for the night. Satar agreed, and he and his friends opened their huge wings and flew into the night. After they left, I told the others that I had found something great that Doc had done for us.

"So come on, everyone, and follow me to the helm. We will make some popcorn, and I will show you what I found."

"Open viewer, Computer. Give us a list of subjects to choose from."

"Okay, Orian," the computer replied. Then the viewer had a big list of all of Doc's projects, of everything from the entire Internet, of every book ever made, and of every movie and song that was on Earth. The one I was going to open was the one that said, "Kids family."

"Look, guys, it's our parents. Ya, that is Mom and Dad," Beth said. "Let's play the videos. How did Doc get all these interactive videos?"

"Each of you put on the glasses in front of you. Then tell the computer to run your program." The girls did, crying, but us guys were strong and didn't cry (yeah right). I told them that Doc had hundreds of bands that people had put around their heads. Then Doc copied all their emotions and feelings; Luke, Shane, Amanda, and Beth could talk to their parents any time they wanted.

"Doreen, I had the computer make you something for your house, and it is being installed as we speak. You and I will go to the house tomorrow, and I will show you the present it made for you."

"Thank you, Orian," Doreen said. "But right now, I want to talk to my parents through the video screen."

As I was serving popcorn, I told the group that, any time they wanted to watch a movie, they should do it in their rooms on the on-screen videos installed in each bedroom and each room in the starship. I knew that the experience would be tough on the kids, so I left them alone. Then I went to my room where I could still access my computer.

As I was sitting in my room talking to Doc on the computer, the computer said that it had analyzed the plasma door and taken samples and scans that we had collected as we had gone through the doorway. The computer told me to be prepared for anything that might happen as we encountered more aliens. I called upon Luke to come to my room and discuss how, when, and where we should arm the humanoids. The computer analyzed the doorway and has strengthened our force fields as we've had problems on this new world.

The next morning when we all got up, I told my friends that Luke, Shane, and I were going into Satar's world.

"The computer has programmed our belts to be able to enter their world without the use of their so-called ring. I want all of you to put your guns on stun, and we will enter today. I have a gut feeling that the Anomies and Leamarkes are fighting today.

"When I talked to Tara, even though he has not visited our new home, he seemed like a very nice creature. The one thing we have to worry about is if our technology is better than others. In these worlds, we should not help to develop weapons to help one side or the other. There may be a little fighting. If we get fired upon, then you have permission to fire back.

"Doreen, and you, Amanda, and you too, Beth—do any of you girls want to come with us? Beth, I thought you might want to check out the plant life, because you like farming so much. and Amanda, would you like to look at all of the different constellations?"

It could be dangerous to take some logging equipment with us as well and go deep into the forests where we would collect a lot of firewood for bonfires.

"Yes. I would love to go," Beth said.

"Me too," said Amanda.

"What about you, Doreen? What are your plans?"

"I think I will finish the house," said Doreen.

"Luke, come with me to the shuttle bay," I said. I looked at Shane. "How is your arm?" I asked him.

"It doesn't hurt a bit," he said.

"That is great," I said. "You feel like coming, Shane?"

"Let me go to the doctor first to see if I can get this cast off."

"Go, Shane, it will take a while for us to get ready to go anyway."

Then Luke and I got twenty humanoids—numbered one through twenty—and I also had my personal humanoid, Mark. Luke and I got the shuttles ready to go and made sure that everything was in operating order.

"Computer," I said, "did you make the modifications to our force fields?"

"Yes, I did, Orian," the computer answered.

"Luke, do you know that your belt has a better force field than before?"

"Yes, I do," Luke said. Like I have mentioned before, Luke was the brilliant one. For his age, he was way ahead of his time. I think that he got that from Doc.

We had two of the humanoids driving the tree harvester, and we would be able to get fifteen to twenty cords, which would last quite a while, inside the machine. I just hoped we didn't get in a fight with the Leamarkes for cutting down some potential homes. We had a new kind of chainsaw that would work well on the trees, and I could turn my weapon into a great plasma beam that would slice through anything.

I asked Luke to go get the rest of the people who wanted to go with us.

"Right now, the only one missing is Shane," Luke said. "Everyone else here, and Doreen has been working on our house."

Then I saw Shane.

"Shane, are you coming with us?"

"I changed my mind," Shane said.

"Why did you change your mind?" I asked.

"I just got my cast off. Plus I want to help Doreen on the house and protect her and the ship while you are gone. Please bring me back a video of your ventures today."

"No problem," I told Shane.

"Luke, did I ever tell you about all the wars that were fought between all these gateways to different worlds?" I asked.

"No, you haven't, Orian."

"Well, I will explain to you on our way to Satar's world."

Then off we went. The machinery was behind us in four small starships with force fields on full and all weapons charged. Soon, we came to the gateway.

I told Luke that I had a token to get into the world, but that our computer had found a way to disable the plasma field and leave it open for good.

"What do you think Luke?" I asked.

"I know you're my older brother, Orian, but they gave you a token that will lead through the plasma. We should use that instead of permanently disabling their defense."

"Amanda, you will love the stars in this new world. Even with all the probes we sent out for billions of years, the constellations from this planet we're going to go to are not in our charts. Don't get scared when you see the Anomies or the large animals that I saw," I said. "Let's go, you guys."

I held the token up that Satar had given me, and the gateway opened, so away we went with our starships, machinery, and humanoids. This gave a big surprise to the guard by the gate. I told him that we meant no harm and that I had talked with Satar. Amanda and Beth and even Luke were in awe when we entered the new world.

By the time we got to Satar's home, they were fighting already, so right away we were in the crossfire of a battle between the Anomies and the Leamarkes.

I told the humanoids with the logging machinery to go deep into the woods beyond the fighting and get us some good firewood and timber. "The hardwood trees are the ones that are red at the base with lush green blossoms that serve as leaves," I said.

"Luke," I said, "let's stop this fight before it gets too bloody for both sides. Sound like a plan?"

We landed our space shuttles. Anomies took the first shot at the shuttle, and force fields held well.

"Please stop fighting," I yelled. "Let's talk about this."

"Too late," Satar said. "The Anomies attacked us last night and killed several of our people."

"Is that true, Tara?" I asked.

"No, it wasn't us," said Tara.

Satar saw me talking to Tara and thought that I was making a deal with him, so Satar started firing at our humanoids and our ship.

"Satar, what are you doing? I'm just talking to Tara, and he said he didn't attack you last night."

"One of our guards saw them."

Tara yelled back and said they were deep in the jungle hunting when the Leamarkes were attacked.

That didn't seem to make Satar want to stop. He kept firing both at us and the Anomies,

"What we do now?" Luke asked me. "Do we defend ourselves or just leave and go deep in the jungle to meet up with the humanoids?"

"Let's give a little taste of our medicine first," I said.

Luke and I got our stun guns and set them not to kill anyone, just to put them asleep for a few hours.

"Satar, quit firing upon us," I yelled. "We're friends."

But that did not stop Satar and his group of soldiers. We had no choice but to fire back. We fired at the Leamarkes but the stun setting didn't faze them, so I set the stun guns to maim, and then I fired. Down one went. I was surprised by how effective their firepower was. Our shields were down to five percent.

"Mark, take readings of the firepower so we can make changes to our force fields."

"Already done," Mark said, "I can make the changes until we get back to the main starship."

The humanoids just stood there and fired their phasers on maim. The Leamarkes were falling one by one.

"They will be just fine," I told Satar. "Your soldiers are only sleeping. Please stop firing. We do not want to go to war with your people. We're trying to unite our planet and your planet, and maybe in time, all planets will be united."

"Never," Satar said as he fired more at our shields.

Our shields were going down as their weapons hit us. But as fast as our phasers could shoot at such a wide angle, we had the upper hand. Finally, Satar quit shooting at us. *Thank goodness*, I thought. *What if our force fields had failed?*

I asked Tara to shoot his weapon at our starship.

"Why?" he asked. "Because I want to see how much damage you can do."

Tara shot his most powerful weapon at us and— *Bam*—our shields went down to twenty percent.

"Did you get that reading, Mark?"

"Yes, I did, Orian, and I will adjust everything when we get back to the starship tonight."

"Tara, we're going deep into the woods today. Is that where your home is?"

"Yes, Orian."

"You better show us, Tara, so we don't cut down some of the vegetation that you might be using."

We hovered over the Anomies and told them to lead the way, and off we went. Satar looked very disappointed.

"Tara, why do you fight with the Leamarkes so much?" I asked.

"We used to be friends," said the Anomies, "but ever since the Leamarkes starting getting attacked every night and he thought it was us, we have been at battle. The battle has been bloody for both sides," he told me. I learned to respect Tara, and Tara went on to say how they had all live on the ground together and watched each other's back. "But it has been a bloody war, Orian, and I hope it ends soon. That will happen when we finally get rid of the Leamarkes altogether," Tara said.

"Tara, you can't go around destroying civilizations. You have to learn how to make peace. On our planet, Earth, in one war, there was a people called the Jews. There was a country called Germany that tried to dominate the whole world, and they thought that Jews were not a pure human person. So they gathered up all the Jews and killed over six million and almost wiped out a complete civilization of Jews," I said. "Let me talk to Satar, and we will see if we can make a peace agreement again at my location, which will be neutral territory, and let's stop the bloodshed."

"I am willing to make peace, if Satar will."

"Then we'll work on that, Tara, okay?"

"Okay, Orian. You set it up."

I radioed the humanoids in the lumber machines and asked them if they were coming.

"We have two loads already finished," the humanoids said.

"When you are finished, find our signal and meet up with us."

"Okay," said the humanoids.

We finally made it to Tara's home.

Tara's people lived in little grass huts piled one on top of the other with ladders going to the top units. They had stores where they could buy supplies. They had weapons factories.

"Tara, how many people do you have living in this large city," I asked.

"Around one million Anomies," Tara said.

"Wow," Luke said.

Tara took us to his home, where we were greeted by his family. Little furry animals were running all over the place, and it kind of looked like a teddy bear factory. I laughed inside my head. These people were smart, but I was surprised that there were not more intelligent life-forms on that planet.

All of a sudden we got a call from the humanoids with the logging machines.

"We are under attack," they said. "Can you help us, Orian?"

"What are you getting attacked by?" I asked.

"By some creature that is the same size as our logging machines," the humanoids said.

"We will be right there," I said. "Tara, do you want to come with us to fight the beasts? Grab your weapons, Tara, and get into the starship, and we'll leave right away. Are you coming, Luke?"

"I wouldn't miss it for the world," Luke said.

Off we went at a tremendous speed, and we got to the humanoids quickly. Sure enough, there were creatures the size of tanks. They had large bodies like an elephant's and heads like a hammerhead shark's.

"What are these creatures called?" I asked Tara. He was hiding behind one of the seats.

"Your weapons will be useless against this creature," Tara said. "It is called a grunt, and it has skin like the mountains on your planet."

"We'll see about that," I said. "Luke, open fire. Use a lazerpon torpedo."

Luke fired one lazerpon torpedo, and a beast was destroyed. The loud blast scared the other ones away. I sent four of my humanoids out to gather the meat from the beast and told them to put the meat on top of the lumber wagons.

"We should hurry up and go back to the portal and get to the starship and put the meat in the freezers. Doreen will help," I said. "Luke, you will talk to Satar and see if we can get a meeting tonight at our new home? Tell him that Tara and his friends will be there as well and that we will talk peace."

While we were exploring in the woods, I saw many tiny creatures that attacked our ship. By then our shields were back up to 100 percent, and we'd had no problems so far. I looked out in the distance and saw funny-looking creatures that were similar to monkeys but walked on two feet and could climb trees. The humanoids and I flew to where we saw the monkey-like creatures. We took video of the creatures, and as we got closer, we saw that they were also very furry. At night, they would look like Anomies just because of their fur color and three shiny eyes.

As we got closer to these creatures, they open fired on our ship and tried to jump on the ship like they were going to take us hostage. Our force fields held somewhat, though the enemies had powerful weapons. When their light beams hit the ship, our force fields would drop by at least 5 percent. Of course, Mark was checking the readings of the weapons.

"I think I solved Satar's problem," I said, and I headed straight for Satar's home. As soon as I got there, I met with Luke and Satar. I showed them the new video of the monkey-like creatures.

"I think that they are the ones doing the fighting with you at night." I said. "Satar, you have to believe me. Tara's people said they never would have attacked you. They have only attacked when you have fired upon them. But these creatures seem to destroy anything or anyone that approaches them."

"I have never seen these creatures before, and I don't know where they came from."

"Let me fly back to Tara, because he wants to meet with you tonight at my place for dinner. He is going to bring some guards as well, so I think you should too. But no weapons will be allowed inside our compound."

"Yes, I will go," Satar said. "And you actually killed this beast?"

"Yes," I said. "And that is what we'll have for dinner tonight," I added with a smile.

I had forgotten that Tara was with me, sitting in my starship.

"Let me go get him, Satar," I said.

"Okay," Satar said.

I went to the starship and got Tara. He walked very cautiously toward Satar. Finally, the two met and talked about old times and actually did some laughing together. I told them that, at dinner tonight, we would figure out a way to beef up their defenses against this new enemy.

"Sounds like a plan," Satar said.

"Satar, look at Tara and tell him you're sorry."

"I did think it was you all this time, but now it looks like we have to work together so they don't get to your villages as well."

"Will you both come together, as one, to dinner tonight? When the sun reaches the mountains, it will be time for dinner. But if you to want to come sooner, I can show you around our starship, and you can look at some of our Earth logs and how we lived."

They responded with no hesitation, "We will be there."

Luke and I say good-bye to Tara and Satar, and we took off through the portal and closed it behind us. Then we headed for the shuttle bay, and as we arrived, we hovered over the new house. We saw that Shane had already started a bonfire; I really thought that Shane missed the farm back home. Luke, on the other hand, and Beth were just excited to be there. Don't get me wrong, I thought it was a beautiful world and I was going to enjoy researching every inch of every planet that was through all those portals, but I did miss home.

Eventually, the humanoids had all the meat put in the freezer, and it was all frozen already. I told the computer to make a meal that the Leamarkes would like.

"We should take some of the meat out of the freezer and see what this new beast we killed today tastes like. We will have to get used to new foods and live on this planet and start the human race all over again," I said. "I just hope that we will not try to dominate over these other intelligent beings."

Shane was the barbecue master. He rotated the meat over the fire he had started. We watched as the meat cooked, and to our amazement, it smelled fantastic.

Then Satar, Tara, and their guards were at the gate of our force field. I asked them if they had any weapons on them. They said no, so I told them they were more than welcome to come in to our home.

"You're just in time. Get ready to eat dinner."

Doreen had done a beautiful job with both the inside of the house and the outside where we could barbecue, eat, and just sit and look at the stars as we talked and sang along with each other or think of the life we had on Earth.

There was a little tension between the Anomies and the Leamarkes, but as time went on, things turned out for the best.

"Ding, ding," Shane said finally. "The meat is done; dinner is ready to be served."

The humanoids brought the meals out to the Leamarkes and asked them if they wanted to try some grunt meat.

"Just a little bit," Satar said. "We are used to all ferns and plant life to eat."

"And that is what we prepared for you Leamarkes for your dinner tonight. I think you will like how it was prepared."

Of course, Anomies loved to eat meat whenever they got a chance.

We all ate, and the grunt meat was fantastic.

After we all ate dinner, I invited our company to our viewing room, and I played a movie to see how they would enjoy it. But what they enjoyed most was the history of our planet and how we lived. I showed them some of the archives of the great battles we had been in and of how our technology had grown over the years. I also showed them encounters we had had with alien life on different worlds as we searched for a planet to live on.

It was getting late as we were showing our company the starship and some of its cargo. They were amazed. I told them to come back again, and then we would join them soon to beef up their defenses against the tree creatures. Then the Leamarkes flew away, and the Anomies headed back on foot.

When I was alone at last, I asked Mark the humanoid to download all the information he had gathered while we were being attacked.

"Already done," Mark said.

"Thank you, Mark. Will we have the results back tomorrow?"

"We should," Mark said. "I will work on them tonight, and by morning, everything should be updated. I will also make the starship's hard drive larger so we can store more data and maybe fix the problem from when we were attacked."

"Mark, you act so concerned for us; it is almost like you are really human."

"Thank you," Mark said. "Your father programmed only two of us humanoids to act similar to him and to always take care of you children the same way that your father would have."

Finally, it was dark outside. All of us were getting tired of six days of straight sunshine and then only thirteen hours of darkness. But I loved the darkness, and everything glowed so prettily. All the plant life came alive. As I watch meteor showers go by, I made a wish—whether it would come true or not, I didn't know.

Then Doreen joined me, and we were both looking out the viewer and watching everything come to life. We were both tired, but we decided to go back down to the livestock area where Amanda and Beth were already.

"What are you doing down here?" Doreen asked.

"Probably the same thing you are doing down here," Beth said.

"Come here, Orian," Amanda said. "Look how fast the livestock is growing, and we just put the eggs in a fluid a day ago."

"I see that," Doreen said.

Then my humanoid, Mark, said, "This fluid is like a big growth hormone and will create a full animal within a week's time."

"What will we feed them Mark?"

"While the other humanoids were putting up our defense fences, they found long bamboo-like trees that are very high in protein and can be chopped down and made into feed. There's enough foliage and insects that the chickens running wild will have plenty of eggs. One does not have to worry about feeding the chickens."

"Oh boy," Amanda said. "Real eggs instead of artificial ones from the computer."

"I will do the milking when the cows come of age and have calves," Beth said.

"Doreen," I said, "your gift will be ready tomorrow."

"Thanks, Orian. I can't wait. Tell me where it is."

"Not until tomorrow, Doreen. I just hope you have room. And our new house! Just think, by tomorrow night, we can start sleeping in our own home. You did a fantastic job, Doreen. And so did the humanoids."

Beth asked me if I had seen our garden.

"I didn't look, Beth," I said.

"This soil is fantastic," Beth said. "The corn is only a month old and ready to be harvested soon—both sweet corn and corn for our cattle. There is cabbage in the garden the size of our kitchen table."

"You're kidding, Beth!"

"No, I am not, Orian, and the carrots are already to eat. They are about five feet long. We have cucumbers, pickles, large watermelon . . . and the fruit trees I planted are already eight feet tall and have blossoms on every branch."

"Great," I said.

Amanda spoke up, "I like to can. I used to help my mother."

"Me too," Beth said. "So both of us can do the canning, Amanda."

"With the days so long here, Computer, how often can we plant our garden?"

"The way this orbit is around our sun," Mark replied instead of the computer, "I believe you can plant year-round, but make sure you do crop rotation, because I would like to see our world use natural fertilizers instead of our computer-made chemical fertilizers."

We were all tired and finally decided to go to our rooms and get some sleep since we had darkness. The computer said that we wouldn't age much on the planet because of its rotation and its spot in the vast universe. The reason I thought about that is because the days were so long, and I wondered if we'd eventually evolve and be able to stay awake for the whole duration of the long sunlight and days. I thought, *tomorrow we will gather some humanoids and we will put up a defense shield around the Leamarkes land and defend the Anomies as well.*

I could have slept forever, but Luke woke me up and said, "Orian, you have to get up and see the sunrise."

"Okay," I said. "Luke, I'll be there in a minute. Let me get my robe." Then I opened up my viewer screen in my bedroom, and the rising sun was a purplish yellow color. It was still dark enough that all plant life was still full of color, and the sky was blue but dusty.

I hurried and woke up Doreen. I told her the same thing Luke had told me, and she opened her viewer and was amazed.

"Luke, since you are so full of energy already, go wake up the others and show them the view."

As we all looked at the beautiful sight that morning, we knew we had a long day—or should I say, days—ahead of us.

"Luke, I want you to take at least twenty humanoids with you and a couple of supply ships full of defensive fencing and make sure that the Anomies have a good defense system against the monkey-looking people. Shane would like to come this time, so hopefully, we'll get them done before nightfall, because the people on their planet only have ten hours of daylight and twenty hours of night. By the time we get ready and get over to the portal, it should be dawn on planet Tuare. Okay, everyone, let's eat breakfast now. I have already sent the humanoids down to the loading bay to get the cargo ships ready to go."

"Why we don't open up some of the other portals?" Luke asked. "We know how to get through the plasma field and keep the portals open and check on those new worlds now."

"Let's get finished with planet Tuare first and do an upgrade on all our defenses. Finish your house, Doreen," I laughed.

While we were eating breakfast, I asked Mark to program a computer to make another 5 percent to 100 percent more new humanoids.

"Orian, before I can make that many new humanoids," the computer said, "you have to send down the mining equipment and some humanoids to bring some rocks from the top of the mountain. I need to fill the cargo bays full of organic material or any kind of mineral. Then I can create anything."

"Fine," I said. "Computer, activate humanoids five through to sixty-five and send them with the mining equipment to get our resources."

"Good idea. Computer, engage . . ."

After we all ate breakfast, we went to our workstations and started getting ready for the projects that we had planned for the day.

First, I showed Doreen her surprise. I walked her down to the house and showed her the viewer screens that I had created for her and for all of us to be able to contact our families, or at least their memories and personalities, whenever we wanted to. Doreen and the other girls started to cry. This was a large project that I had made for our new home. It was designed to be accessed from every room, with a large monitor inside as well as one outside. I had had the humanoids work overtime to get it completed during our thirteen hours of sleep. The girls loved it.

In the cargo bay, the humanoids had all the ships loaded full of equipment and supplies that we needed for the day's work.

"Shane, I think I will let you take care of Satar's defenses," I said, "and I am going to take one of the starships around this world. I will take twenty humanoids with me, fully armed, to see what other dangers lurk in this new world. I don't think planet Tuare is as peaceful as the Anomies and the Leamarkes say it is. Just visiting the desert on Earth, there were living creatures, like scorpions, snakes, and other underground creatures. And on this planet, everything is large, and there seems to be an abundant water supply coming from somewhere. I plan to find out more today about this planet Tuare, maybe somehow see if the world we live on has anything to do with the weather or water supplies for the planets in each portal.

"Luke, you ready? Shane, are you all set? Amanda, Beth, will you take care of the animals today? Doreen, will you keep in touch with the humanoids that are doing the mining?"

"Sure, Orian, I will keep them on the video screen at all times."

"Thanks, Doreen, and while the humanoids are being made, make sure that they go back to the mining operation and have both the cargo bay and the mining equipment full of material we might need for future operations. Thank you, Doreen. You have been wonderful in all your projects, and thank you," I said. "Well, guys, let's get going. We'll see you girls. Be back in thirteen hours, and thanks for packing lunch."

Then off we went, soaring into the sky. Within minutes we were at the portal. I used the computer's programming to enter the portal this time, and when we entered, I started toward where the Leamarkes had their landmass. All we saw was death and destruction—not just the Leamarkes but the Anomies as well. It looked like they had fought side-by-side against a common enemy.

I saw Satar. His wings were badly damaged. I asked what had happened, and Satar told me how the Leamarkes and the Anomies had all been gathered together, talking about peace when the attack had started. The monkey people had come from every direction. They had stormed the camps, climbed the trees to get to the Leamarkes, and just started to use their weapons on women and children and the soldiers.

"Where is Tara?" I asked.

"Over by the river. They're gathering bodies to burn in a remembrance ceremony for the dead," Satar said.

"Satar, I will go over and talk to Tara. I'm leaving my brother Shane here to put up defenses for the people you have left, and we're doing the same for Tara and the other Anomies, putting up defenses around his village."

Satar said that a lot of his soldiers and family members had gotten away by flying.

"Well, Satar, they will be safe tonight," I said. "Shane, do the best you can do here. Get the humanoids working on the fence, and show Satar how to use the controls so their kind can get in and out. This is a different frequency of force field from ours, so no one can get past your defenses. But we can access all defenses we are putting here. Well, I'll see you later Shane. I am going to talk to Tara and tell them all how sorry I am. Then I will see how Luke is doing, putting defenses around that large village, and I will show everyone the video of the desert and other parts of the world that I see here today. Everyone make sure you have your force fields on. And have your phasers set to kill if the monkey people come back," I said.

"Hey Tara, I just left Satar, and he told me what happened. I am sorry. If I only knew, we could have helped. Luke is in your village right now with several of my humanoids, fully armed, and putting up defenses for your people. But I have to go, Tara. I think there are more dangers for you out there in that large desert. But, Tara, you said you didn't have any enemies besides the Leamarkes until I found the monkey people with very strong weapons, and you said you'd never seen them before, right?"

"You're right, Orian. They may have come across the desert if they found water someplace."

"I will check this out today, Tara. But keep your men prepared to fight at all times. Though not against the Leamarkes; they're on your side now. I think, together, your people can defeat the enemy. Tara, with our advanced computer system, we are able to go through your portal and the other portals without your permission, but we still ask. Someday, I hope to have all portals left open. That way, if we need people or other aliens we are at peace with, maybe someday we can all fight the same battle together.

"Well, off I go, Tara, I will check with you on the way back from the desert and the other side of your world."

Then with a loud whoosh I was off, flying through the jungle plants. They changed shapes and sizes as I approached the desert. Then just like that, I was over pure sand. It looked like the Sahara desert. I had the scanner on full to check for a life-forms, and the computer was set to pick up voices and translate to our language if aliens were saying anything.

I started to pick up a lot of life signs, and when I did, I slowed the starship down and circled where the life-forms were. Some of life-forms I encountered were very dangerous; they were camouflaged to look like the sand, and if anything walked over it, a mouth would open up and swallow its prey whole. As I got deeper in the desert, I found small twenty-four-legged creatures that could move as fast as a leopard. I encountered creatures with tentacles all around them that seemed to catch anything that either flew near them or landed on them. I took samples of over twenty-five different creatures just in one hour—the desert was truly alive.

I decided to gain altitude and map the planet. The higher I got, the more I could tell that the desert got rain often. There were a lot of washed-out dunes that could only have been shaped by water. Then, a little farther inland, there was a lake. I landed next to the lake and got out of my ship. I took Mark with me, and we took samples of the water. To my surprise, it was made of the same minerals as we found in the ocean on the planet that we lived on. Somehow the force in the center of our world must have been control water in this world. All around the lake was lush green vegetation, and I had had to cut down some with the knife just to get to the lake.

Then out of the blue, a vine grabbed my leg and started pulling me toward a big flower. My humanoid Mark was right there, and he took his phaser out and cut the vine that was holding my leg. My leg was all black and blue, and the vine had seemed to want to dig into my leg. Mark and I walked over by a huge white flower, and more vines tried to grab our legs. Mark picked me up and carried me out of danger's way.

As we explored the watery area and took samples of the vegetation, there were tree-like ferns with very hard, timber-like trunks. Then Mark and I went back into our starship with the other humanoids. We were just sitting there; we seemed to be waiting for a fight if we were to meet any enemies in the desert.

Just as I got up into the air and had gone a little farther inland—I figured I was three to four hundred miles into the desert—all of a sudden, I saw ant-like creatures coming out of a distant wood ahead of us. They were chewing down trees with big incisor-filled mouths. I zoomed forward and stopped within a good viewing distance. As I watched them eat the forest right to the ground, I saw that these creatures had about ten legs and could really move. I watched as one of the large, ant-like creatures cut a huge tree down with his incisors. He held it in his mouth. It must have weighed at least two tons.

I must have stayed there for an hour, watching the huge creatures devour that whole forest. Then one finally looked up at me. It must have set off an alarm for the rest of them. I started getting strong electrical bolts shot at my starship. This time, the force fields held. I thought I would test out the strength of my phaser, so I shot one with a medium-strength beam, and it just kind of bounce off his hard armor.

Then I saw the creatures enter the desert and start heading toward where the Leamarkes and Anomies live. I had to get back to the Anomies and the Leamarkes. At the rate that these large, ant creatures were traveling, I figured we had four days to stop them. We would have to fight them at the line between the trees and the desert.

I set my starship's speed at nine hundred miles an hour and was with in the Anomies and Leamarkes in no time. Tara was still working on gathering bodies. The Leamarkes were finished with their dead, so I talked to Satar and told him about the creatures that were coming their way. I told Satar that we would have to work day and night to put up more force fields at the edge of the desert and the forest.

"The humanoids will be finished with your layer today. My computer is making another two hundred humanoids that will assist us in the fight at our side, Satar," I said. "I must talk to Tara and see how many of his people he can spare to help stop this destruction."

I showed Satar the video of the creatures, and I told the Leamarkes that they would have the advantage because they could fly and attack from above.'

I went to see Tara, and I showed him the same video.

"This may be the end of days for people," he said.

"Tara," I said, "we are here to help you." I told him about putting defenses up between the desert and the vegetation. Then I instructed the humanoids to take the supply ship back to the main starship and reload it. That would be all of the force field defenses that we had.

"You have to tell the computer in the starship to create at least two loads of force field fences," I said. "That means the mining of ore will have to continue day and night to keep the starship full of material to create humanoids and fencing. Luke, Shane, when you're done, bring your starships back to base camp. Luke, you fly high in the air. Go straight to the desert, and you'll see what I'm talking about. Then turn your starship around and come home so we can all make decisions on how to fight.

"Tara, I know you have a burial celebration tonight," I continued, "but can you and Satar stop at my place tonight so we can all make a plan?"

"This is a sad day for us as well, but I will come," Satar said.

"I trust Satar, so you and Satar make the plans, and we will help," said Tara. "But tonight we have to mourn."

I called Satar over, and I told him that, when he and the humanoids were finished, he should come back with them, and then we would draw out a plan.

"First, we might have to fight the monkey people just to get to the edge of the forest. But maybe if the monkey people see the threat we have, they might switch over to our side. I wouldn't trust them, but they sure could help us. In fact, Satar, I am going to confront the monkey people right now and show them the threat that is coming."

"You can try," Satar said, "But I won't stand side by side with those people after what they've done to us."

"Maybe to fight with us," I said, "but I would tell them never to attack you again."

I climbed back into my starship and asked Mark to check for life signs as we fly through the canopy of the forest. We took off headed toward where we saw the monkey people before, but they were nowhere to be found. I flew east; I flew west.

Finally, Mark said, "I have them just one klick away."

We slowed to a stop in front of the monkey people. They were still celebrating after their victory the night before.

"Where is your leader?" I yelled out.

"Who wants to know?"

"I do, and my name is Orian. I'm from a different planet. The people you slaughtered last night were my friends," I said. "I feel like just killing you all with one blast."

That got their attention, and all of them tried to fire their weapons at my shuttle, but my force fields held. I set my phasers to kill and shot one of the monkey people. That got their attention once again.

"Now will you listen to me?" I asked.

"Yes," said a very large, black-and-white monkey with big white ears. He stood on his hind legs and gave me a dirty look.

"What are you called?" I asked.

"Toco," he said.

"Well, Toco. You better come over and see this. Your life is in danger and not from us; we are a peaceful people, but we protect our friends. There are large, ant-like creatures coming our way, and they will be here within three days. We all have to join forces to fight them. Their armor is tough, but it can be pierced."

I showed Toco the video of the creatures that were coming our way. I told Toco that if he could fight in a separate location from us, the Anomies, and the Leamarkes would take over another location.

"If we survive this battle, I will make sure that there is peace between all creatures on this side of the planet," I said.

I still didn't trust the monkey people or creatures, but if they could fight at one end of the line, then with everyone fighting together, the Anomies, the Leamarkes, and the monkey people might have peace afterward. But for the moment, the Anomies and the Leamarkes were safe as long as they stayed in their barriers.

I left to go back home to start to make a strategy map. I had the main layout of the area from pictures that I took from the air, and I'd send the humanoids in that night to start putting up a force field fence. We would fly during the day to see how far the ant creatures had advanced. I knew they would stop at the water, and Luke, Shane, and I would take separate starships and give them a surprise attack at the watering hole. We might be able to get enough of them to maybe turn them around.

I finally made it back to the shuttle bay and parked my starship. I asked my twenty humanoids to get out and go to the Humanoid bay to help the computer speed up the development of new humanoids that would need to fight the ant-like creatures.

Then I went down to the house and met the girls. I told them what was happening on planet Tuare. They were surprised and shocked. I told them that we had fences around Satar's people's homes and that the Anomies' village was protected now. I told the girls that when we had gotten there, it had been a bloody mess. The monkey people had attacked during the night and pretty much won the battle.

I had Mark download all the videos onto the computer mainframe so I could show the girls the threat we were facing.

"Doreen, I know you don't like me to fight," I said, "but this is one that I have to do. I defend my friends, and we might be living on these different worlds someday."

I told the girls about my plan to ambush the ant creatures the next day at the watering hole. I told them that our force fields had held through very well in the attack that we got from the ant creatures that day. I also told the girls of a deal made with the monkey people; they would fight from one side of the forest while the Anomies and the little Leamarkes and we would take the middle and the ends.

"Satar will be here later today," I said. "He has already buried his dead, so he will be here planning our attack on the ant people. Doreen, Amanda, and Beth, would you like to go with some humanoids to the funeral ceremonies at the Anomies village tonight?"

"Oh sure, we would Orian. We would be glad to represent you, if you like."

"You have done so much for them already, Doreen,"

"Yes, Orian."

"When you go tonight, activate humanoid number one hundred and ninety-nine, and her name is whatever you want it to be. The computer said she is a special humanoid that will keep you and the other girls safe while you attend the ceremony. And Doreen, I told the computer that you would make her special, and she will have your mother's voice."

Doreen named her new humanoid Sara, so now Sara is her name.

"She will be your personal humanoid from now on, and you will be surprised how well she knows you and all of us. Take good care of her," I said. "Computer . . ."

"Yes, Orian?"

"How are we coming with the humanoids?"

"Fine, Orian, I have built five percent so far, and they are in the programming stage right now. The other humanoids brought us more than enough ore from the mountains to make the fences you will need for protection.

I sent two humanoids back for one more shipment of ore.

"Orian, I also made special suits for you, Luke, and Shane to wear. When you go into battle, if the force field fails, the suit I designed should still protect you and the humanoids. They have advanced weaponry and will help you when you go into battle in a couple days."

"Computer," I said.

"Yes, Orian?" the computer asked. "What can I do for you now, Orian?"

"Well, Computer, remember what Doc said about the ship being able to hold over one thousand five hundred people?"

"Yes, I remember," the computer said.

"Computer, we only have four starships in the shuttle bay. I will keep other humanoids making more, but by the end of the month, is it possible to have a hundred starships in the shuttle bay? It is a tall order."

"Orian, yes it is."

"Computer, I might teach the humanoids how to fly the starships. I know Mark and you have the capability of teaching others how to fly missions and do well in combat."

"That is true, Orian; the humanoids have emotions like humans and can figure out ways to get out of critical situations, just like a smart human could."

"Computer, keep building humanoids until we have enough to fly all the starships we'll have in the shuttle bay."

"If that is your wish, Orian."

"Yes, it is, Computer. And computer, can you make them personal, like humanoid one twenty-seven and humanoid one ninety-nine?"

"To make that happen, Orian, I will have to ask your humanoid Mark or humanoid one ninety-nine to transfer some of their emotions and brainpower to these other humanoids."

"Make it so, Computer. In two days, how many humanoids can we make and get programmed?"

"Orian, we should have another hundred to program in two days. The starships will take longer, but in a month . . . well, actually, in a month on this planet, I should have one hundred new starships made, but we will have to keep the material coming in from the mountains."

"I'm just nervous, Computer. I wish Doc was here. He would help us defend our friends a lot easier."

"Orian, Satar is coming, and he is a warrior, and so is Tara. Satar is here now, Orian."

"Thanks, Computer. I will let him in."

I went down the elevator to the first floor of the starship, stepped out, took a left turn, and walked out of the starship. I had the humanoids open the gate, and I greeted Satar and his friends

"Let's get busy planning our attack and offenses and defenses," I said. "Satar you and your friends come with me."

We all walked into the starship and got in the elevator, which took us to the humanoid-making bay. When they saw the operation with all of the humanoids coming off the production line, they were very impressed.

"We will have a lot of manpower, and with our starships, we will defeat these ant creatures.

I told Satar about the deal I had made with the monkey people. He was mad at first, but I told him it was their lives too. The more that we had a fight with, the better chance we had to win.

Satar agreed, but he said, "If we defeat these large creatures, what shall we do about the monkey people?"

"Satar," I said, "that is up to you and Tara. You have to live in that world, and if you want to fight the monkey people and drive them out of your area, then that's fine with us. I don't blame you if you want revenge, but if they turn out to be peaceful after the war, maybe we can work something out with them. If not, they will have to be destroyed."

"Orian," Satar said, "why are you so worried about our planet and the people in it—or creatures, as you call us?"

"Well, it's like this: you are my friends now, and when we start repopulating this planet, we might have to expand into your planet and other planets through these different portals. We have the technology to turn that desert sand into a fertile planting ground," I said. "Well, there goes one set of defensive force fields. The humanoids will take them into the desert and set up a boundary as far as the eye can see.

"Satar," I continued, "when you and the Leamarkes fly with us to attack from above, please do not get close to our exhaust vents. I don't want to see you getting sucked into our systems. Stay either right below us or off to our side. Then the force field will protect you while you are firing down on the enemy. It will be my pleasure to fly next you, Satar."

"With you as well, Orian."

"Tara and the humanoids will be fighting head-on. They can shoot through our force fields, but the ant-like creatures shouldn't be able to fire back. I think we have a good chance of winning, don't you?"

"Yes, I do, Orian, Especially with you on our side."

As the days went by, the humanoids worked on the force field along the desert and finally got it operational. I introduced the monkey people to the Leamarkes and the Anomies, and they made a peace agreement—at least until the war was over. The only thing that I said was that I would be on Satar and Tara's side.

"Well, people, we are now ready for war. Luke," I called him on the intercom, "how far away is the enemy from the watering hole?"

"Another twenty minutes," Luke said.

"Well, Satar, I'm off now to join Luke and Shane to try to give a good massacre at the watering hole. That should slow them down!"

Off I went in my starship.

Luke, Shane and I flew high so we would not be noticed. In just a few more minutes, they would all be gathered at the watering hole.

"Here they come. Steady, steady. Army tour plan, lazerpon torpedoes."

"We're ready, Orian, you just give us the word."

"Now," I said. "Let's give them some hell."

Down we swooped with our lazerpon torpedoes firing away cluster bombs that landed all around the creatures, exploding and sending pieces of them high in the air.

"There are so many," Luke said.

"Just keep firing," I said. "Put your phaser on a widespread beam and make sure it's set to kill."

We fired off the phasers, killing the ant people left and right. They were fighting back, hurling bolts of lightning at us, hitting our force fields. So far the shields were holding.

"I don't know how much more they can take. Just keep firing," I said. "That is the way, Shane. Keep your phaser on and spread them out."

As we fired, they kept throwing lightning bolts at us. Soon were shields were feeling the pain and slowly fading.

"I still have sixty percent," I said.

"I have five percent," Luke said.

"I'm down to five percent shields," Shane said.

"Take the ships higher, guys, and let the shields recharge."

"Good idea, Orian."

Up we went. We hovered high above the watering hole as millions of ant creatures kept coming.

"How are your shields now," I asked Luke and Shane.

"They're getting better," Luke said.

"Orian, those ant creatures don't seem to move forward much. I think we have them stopped at the watering hole for now, guys," Shane yelled.

"There are just too many of them, Orian."

"We will just have to do the best we can," I said. "All right, you guys. My shields are back at one hundred percent. Lots of phaser power left. How about you, Shane and Luke?"

"About the same as you, Orian."

"Then let's hit them again."

We all got into formation and turned our phasers on widespread beams. We decided to swoop over the entire population of the ant creatures. As we went down for our run, lightning bolts came from all directions, hitting the force fields. Most of the hits bounced off, but still the shields were down to seventy percent.

"Open fire, guys," I said.

We held on our phaser buttons all way down, and we laid out a very wide area of pure phaser beams. They hit the ant creatures right down the middle and killed thousands.

"The lightning bolts have brought my shields down to five percent. How about you, Luke and Shane?" I asked. "How are you holding out?"

"Just about the same, Orian."

"We will have to call off the attack for a while."

"I agree."

"Okay, Orian, we will follow you."

We headed back to the base at Tara's place. After we landed at Tara's base, we were able to watch the battle on the monitors that we had set up in the city streets.

"Satar, I don't know if we can stop them all. We've killed probably one million so far, but they keep on coming. Those lightning bolts will weaken our force fields that we have up. Let's hope your firepower is as strong as ours, so we can hold them at the line. One big mistake I made is that, when I came through the portal, I forgot to shut it down, so the portal is still open. How are the starships looking, Luke? How are the shields? Are the weapon systems charged back up?"

"Not quite yet," Luke said, "but getting there."

"Tara, we might get one more shot at them at the watering hole before we have to let the starships recharge."

"Well, guys, let's all give them one more taste of our guns. Then we will have to prepare for the land battle. That will come either later tonight or first thing tomorrow morning. Let's hope for the latter."

We all got back into our starships and headed back to the watering hole.

"They're still there, right?"

"They are," Luke said. "But this time they are all lined up in a big circle, like they are waiting for us."

"I was afraid of that," I said.

"Stay back quite a distance, and let's shoot some big rays from the lazerpon torpedoes at them," Luke said.

"Good idea, Luke."

We stayed well away from the watering hole as they shot lightning bolts at us. At that distance, the shields held.

"Fire lazerpon torpedoes," I yelled into the microphone, and we all shot at the same time.

"Look at those babies blow," said Shane. "Let's hit them again."

"Fire lazerpon torpedoes at full strength," I said.

We did and took out another few hundred thousand of the enemy, but it still looked like there were millions. We are running low on our lazerpon torpedoes.

"Fire your last lazerpon torpedo," I said.

Off they went directly into the middle. *Bam, boom*— like a big thundercloud, the noise was terrifying.

"I'm out of lazerpon torpedoes, guys. What do you want to do now?"

"Let's put the phasers on a spread pattern," someone said.

We did, and we lined our ships up together and took off toward the main bulk of the enemy with our phasers burning the ground and boiling the water before they hit the enemy. Then it just tore the flesh off the enemies' bodies as we spread through them. The whole time, we were getting hit by strong lightning bolts, and our force fields were just about spent.

"Luke, let's go back to the base and get ready for the ground attack," Shane said.

When we landed back at the base, we told Tara and Satar that we had killed millions of the creatures but that there were still millions more coming.

"I think they will stay at the waterhole tonight and then try to attack us tomorrow. We'll leave the humanoids here and leave the portal door open so you can call us if they decide to strike earlier, but we have to reload our starships for the main battle tomorrow."

"Okay," Tara said. "We will call you if they decide to attack tonight."

Once we were back at home, we were talking to the gals about the battle that we had fought, and I told them that I did not think that we would be able to win the war. I told them I had left the portal open to planet Tuare so Tara or Satar could communicate with us if the ant creatures decided to attack at night.

"But I'm tired," Doreen said. "I had a rough day too. Trying to hook up your video system wasn't the easiest in the world, Orian." She tried to keep a smile on her face. "All that you did today was fight a war with humanoids. I had to work with wires."

"Oh, Doreen. You sound like we're married already! But I love you, Doreen."

Then out of the blue, we heard voices, and they weren't Satar's voice.

"Computer, turn on the floodlights."

"Done," the computer said.

Then we saw the strangest tall green creatures. They were about seven feet tall, but they had small heads, large eyes, and very long fingers.

"Hello," I said. "We are a friendly people who landed on this planet. Where do you hail from?"

"We live on a planet called Saphra, which is just through the portal about a half a mile south of your home. We are also a friendly people. May we come in through your force field and get more acquainted with each other?"

"Sure," I said. "My name is Orian, and yours is . . . ?"

"Loper, and these are my brothers."

"Loper, sit down. All of you. Look at this video and tell me if you have ever seen a creature like this before."

"Yes, on a different planet. These things destroyed almost all living life on that planet."

"Loper, we have friends on a planet through another portal just west of here, and we have been fighting all day with these creatures. Do you know how we can defeat the creatures?"

"Yes," said Loper. "We had to destroy those creatures on our planet just a few years ago."

"We killed many of them today," Luke said, "but the lightning bolts damaged our force fields. There are just too many for the few of us to handle. The people that we are helping do not have that sophisticated of weapons."

"I think that we can help you if you would do us a favor afterwards."

"Name it," I said.

"I saw your humanoids mining today, and you have some pretty sophisticated mining equipment. We have one area that we would like to mine—not much, just enough to keep our reactors going if you wouldn't mind."

"No problem," I said. "We have to act quickly though. I expect an attack by midmorning at the main defense position that we have."

"You have a force field up?"

"Yes, we do, but we don't know how many strikes it can take before it fails."

"I will have one thousand soldiers out here tomorrow morning. Will you be ready?"

"Yes, we'll be ready, and so will the people who are inside. They're"—I pointed indoors—"watching right now to see if they might attack early. I have over one hundred fifty humanoids in there, and I put barriers around each of the peoples' towns to protect them when it comes down to the end."

"With our guns and your guns," Loper said, "we will surely wipe them off that planet for good."

"Oh, thank you," I said. "You don't know how much I need the help. And yes we will mine for you, and you can use my humanoids and machinery until the job is done. Loper, do you mind if we visit your world after we get done fighting side by side tomorrow."

"Yes, you may. We live in a peaceful world and have many people. But we still come to the source in your new land now and then to give our thanks for the water we receive to make our planet thrive."

The next morning, we all got up early, and sure enough, Loper and his troops were waiting by the gate.

"Get ready, guys, we have a war to fight today," I said. "Doreen, you see this button?"

"Yes, Orian, I see it."

"If things go bad, you press that button and close the portal."

"Just be careful, Orian. You too, Luke and Shane."

We opened the gates, and I asked Loper to ride in the starship with me. Loper got in, and off we went to help our friends. All of his troops were in faster transportation, so we were at the portal in no time at all.

As we all came through the portal, Satar and Tara were amazed by all the help that we brought.

"I think we have a fighting chance now," I said. "Come on, let's go up to the frontline, and I'll show you where our defenses are. Satar, Tara, this is Loper. He and his troops have battled these monsters before, and before night falls, your land will be pure again."

"Luke, Shane, let's take our starships in for one last fight before we start our main battle."

Satar, Tara, and Loper entered my starship to get to the main front before the monsters would wake up and decide to attack first. So off we went in our starships.

"Luke, Shane, keep your distance like before—just out of range of their lightning bolts, and we'll rain down on them with our lazerpon torpedoes."

"There they are," said Luke.

"I see them too," said Shane.

"Hold your positions," I said. "Fire."

Twelve lazerpon torpedoes took off all at once toward the ant-like creatures. Then I saw a huge explosion, and I thought we had gotten them all in that one strike.

When the dust cleared, they were all starting to head toward our defense line with about a half hour to get ready.

"Let's spread them with our phasers again, Luke. You ready, guys? Let's spread our phasers out," I said.

Off we went with our phasers blazing away. We went through the center of the pack and spread them out.

"Let's go back to the base now, Luke and Shane."

"Okay, boss," they responded.

We landed our starships and set them to recharge.

Chapter Six

I noticed that Loper's men were all equipped with strange-looking weapons.

"What kinds of weapons are those?" I asked Loper.

"You'll see, Orian. These are the weapons we used when we conquered these beasts that we called Vipeters."

All of the Amonies and the Leamarkes were lined up along the force field defenses and ready for the fight that was coming soon.

I talked to Loper and told him that there were wars among the planets a long time before and that they had made a peace agreement after thousands of years of fighting.

"I didn't know that," Loper said.

"Yes," Satar said. "Many fights. At one time, we were all friends, Loper, so now we all have an agreement not to enter any planet and to respect anything that we encountered at the source for over a thousand years now. On the Grants' new planet, we were all friends at one time, and then war broke out and seemed to spread to all the different planets. Then when so many had died, we made that agreement that I told you about."

"Luke," I called out on the microphone, "how close are the Vipeters to us now?"

"They should be in range in about one hour," Luke said. "I have been giving them short bursts of phaser blasts to keep them at bay. I am going up and out to recharge the force fields and phaser banks, and the lazerpon torpedoes as well."

"Good, Luke. Our ships are all charged up and ready for the big fight," I said. "Luke, I have the computer working—on my ship and Shane's ship and your ship too—to update the force fields and phasers for the coming fight. They will be more effective and will help you not have to get away from the fight to recharge. The computer told me that the force fields will hold now, and if we get short of firepower, we can still fly right through them and kill some of them and scatter the rest.

"Loper," I continued, "before they get in range, we will fly our shuttles to engage the Vipeters in the desert about a quarter of an hour before they are in range."

Loper said that his people were called Slackers. I laughed when he told me the name of his people, and I told him that we called people on Earth slackers when they were lazy. "Lazy people didn't conform to others' will."

Loper laughed.

"Yes, and human in our language means 'farters.'"

We both laughed.

"Hold on, Loper, while I talk to Luke," I said.

Luke asked his computer if the changes had been made, and if so, if we could attack them and try to slow them down.

"Okay, Luke," I said.

Luke said that the computer had made the changes to the force fields and had increased our firepower by

70 percent. "We won't have to recharge our phasers and lazerpon torpedoes as many times as before. We will be able to recharge faster if we get damage to our force fields."

"Very advanced systems you have, Orian," Loper said.

"Yes," Satar said.

"We have seen Orian and the rest fight. People fight to see what their weapons can do so they are ready. They are more advanced than us," Tara said.

"Same here," said Loper, "but we have superior weapons when it comes to fighting the ant people, or the Vipeters, which is what we call them."

"Let's hope that Luke is doing okay."

I watched Luke's video on the big screen.

"Shane, get into your starship and go help Luke. I will join you when they get closer to us. You have an updated system now, but still listen to what the computer tells you. If the shields do get damaged . . . Mark, my personal humanoid told all of us that the shields will hold up to five percent. So get out quick or before you reach that level."

Shane started up his starship, and off he went to join Luke as all of us watched them. Loper then asked Mark and me if the force fields had been updated where his men were staged.

"Let me check, Loper," I said. "Computer, have the force fields been updated where we have placed them on the desert barrier and also around the Leamarkes and the Amonies' homes and cities?"

"Still working on them," the computer said. "While you are fighting, you can just ask your humanoid Mark questions and listen to his advice about what to do. The portal can be shut and nothing can get through it if you ending up losing the battle, but I will keep updating the systems as the force fields get hit." The computer went on to tell us that there was a button on our hand phasers that had to be voice activated in order for us to use the phasers. That button on our phasers would become activated only when we said our names and "Blaster on." That will activate the button that would send out one big blast and only one. Then our phasers would have to recharge. "You should consider leaving the planet and getting everyone out of there," the computer said.

The leaders of the four races were watching the viewer as Luke and Shane went on the offensive and shot phasers at them and some lazerpon torpedoes at them from a distance. They were trying not to get the ships to discharge much energy, but they were shooting enough firepower to slow the Vipeters down. At times, they sent them back toward the lake in the desert. But the Vipeters would soon turn back toward us. There were millions of dead Vipeters all over the ground, but they seemed to have little sense of fear.

"That is how they were in our war as well," Loper said. "And we lost a large number of our people as we fought these monsters that were consuming all plant life on our planet. They seemed to cross our vast oceans, and they consumed plant life and races from all continents. We were the last, and like you, Orian, we had to leave our planet and search for a place where we could start over. But we had several ships and were able to save thousands. We have only been on our new planet for four tenters; I don't know how long that is in your time scale."

"We don't know yet either," I told Loper. "The days are longer here, and the nights are short. So we are still going by our time that we had on Earth . . . until we come up with a new calendar and time information, anyways.

"I thought that you destroyed the Vipeters on your planet," I asked Loper.

"We thought that we did, but all plant life was gone, and with the oxygen quickly depleting and without plant life, we had to leave our planet. We took as many of our people as we could. We left many behind to fight the remaining Vipeters and hoped that they could defeat the beasts.

"Hopefully someday, we can return to our planet if our star charts can lead us back. It has been tenters since we have heard from our lost planet, and it was many generations of our people before we found the planet that we are on now. We have kept a log, like I believe your huge starship did for you, and we traveled in space through many star systems to land where we are now. We have a new home with many new kinds of friendly people on it, and they helped us out as we grew back in numbers.

"But back to the war to come," Loper said. "Our guns are effective, but get ready to leave if our and your defenses fail. And if we run out of firepower, we'll need to get the heck out of here . . . fast!"

"That is the plan," Mark said. "And we will close the portal and come back another time if we decide to fight until they are all destroyed. We humanoids have taken seeds from all of the plant life in the surrounding areas, so if we have to, we can reproduce this world if needed."

"Loper, Satar, Tara, your people are welcome to live on our planet by the source if we need to evacuate and close the portal."

"That is fine for us as long as we can survive with your species."

"Yes," said Loper, "and we have a place for you in our world as well."

"Come on, you guys, we haven't lost yet. But I did notice that the surrounding creatures have disappeared as if they feel that danger is coming.

We watched as Luke and Shane kept on fighting the Vipeters and holding them at bay for the moment. But there just kept on getting to be more and more of them on the sands.

"This doesn't look good," I said. "Satar, Tara, just to be safe, lead your people through the portal to our world, and we will just leave the ones who will fight here."

Mark, my humanoid, interrupted and told us that, if our force fields started to fail, we needed to evacuate at once. Tensions rose as we kept hearing warnings from our computer and all the different plans that we were coming up with between us.

"Hold on," I said. "If we have to evacuate this world, your people, Loper, will go before us. And that is after the Leamarkes and Amonies get out first. They have the least effective weapons. Then your people, Loper, will all line up with us, and we will shoot off our blaster weapons and see what that does. Then we will get out and close the portal."

"Fine."

At least, everyone had agreed on something for if the worst happened.

I told the group that I was going to get into my starship and help Shane and Luke kill as many Vipeters as we could before they hit us at our defense site. Mark and I climbed into the starship, and off we went. Soon we joined the other two starships. I thought just three ships against the whole Vipeters army or race was not enough. Their origin was too confusing, thinking about how they got to this planet in the first place.

"Computer—I mean, Mark. How are we looking on the ground as far as our defenses go?"

"Fine," Mark said. "Everything has been updated with all the data that we have found out so far."

"Well, Mark, it's my turn to take a whack at these ant creatures," I said. "Luke, Shane, are you with me?"

"You bet we are. Let's do it and give them a bloodbath before we have to go to ground fighting."

"Mark, have you and the humanoids on the front line communicated the information on evacuation if we need to?"

"Yes," said Mark. "When I get updated, so do all the humanoids in service."

"Good," I said. "Because the humanoids have feelings like us, and I don't want them to be grieving if we lose a member of our crew or a brother."

"Orian," Mark said, "you are like your father in many ways. You are always thinking of others, no matter what race or people they are. You have met so many different ones so far. I hope that Luke and Shane and the others have that feeling as well."

"I know that Doreen and Amanda have the same feelings, and Beth has to learn to understand more, but she is young and not as advanced as Luke is.

"Shall I give the order to attack?" I asked Mark.

"Go ahead," Mark said.

"Luke, Shane, let's spread out to about a mile or two apart and stay short of the Vipeters lightning bolts or weapons' effective range. Then let's put our lazerpon torpedoes on spread and hit them hard. We will fire five lazerpon torpedoes at a time and then sit and recharge. Maybe one of us will stay at the center, firing and the others can go to each end and fire from both sides."

"Great idea, Orian. Let's line up and get going and kill theses Vipeters."

We all pushed our joysticks forward and got within firing range. We let go fifteen lazerpon torpedoes all at one time. A large blast went across the desert, destroying everything in a large area and killing millions of Vipeters at one time. The sand glowed red hot as the smoke cleared up. It was too hot for the Vipeters to walk on right away, so we hit them hard, and they started to back up and head back toward the lake, either to drink some water or to regroup. But at least we had sent them back miles from the main defense line. It would take them a day to get to our main defenses.

"Lazerpon torpedoes at one hundred percent, and everything ready for another attack," Mark said.

I asked Shane and Luke if they had both reached 100 percent as well.

"Yes," they radioed back.

I radioed Satar and the others.

"Good going," they said. "We are watching. You seem to have given us another day to get ready and to gather people at the evacuation site."

"We have only begun to fight today and will try to drive them back further," I said.

"Then go get them," Loper said. "The more you kill today, the less we will have to kill tomorrow when and if they get to the main defenses."

"Right on," Luke said in a smart tone of voice.

"Cool it, Luke. Let's get closer and hit them again. Then afterward, Shane, you go to the left side of the Vipeters, and Luke, you go to the right, and we will all fire at one time."

We all agreed.

"And don't forget: if we fail, they might find a way to get to our world and destroy us. Maybe not the starship, but at least they might find a way to open the portals and threaten other worlds or planets."

"We know, Orian," Luke said. "We heard most of what you and Loper were talking about when his people were at battle with those beasts, but why can't we read their minds?"

"I don't know, Luke." So I asked Mark. "Mark, why can't we communicate with them and find out what they really want?"

"The computer is working on that," Mark said, "but they have so many different sound waves, it is hard to compute what they are saying."

"That is all fine and well," Shane said, "but let's hit them again and quit fooling around."

"Boy," I said, "who died and left you boss, Shane?"

"Sorry, Orian, but I am kind of scared and want to fight on and just go home if we can."

"Right," I said. "Luke, are you in position?"

"Yes," Luke said.

When we reached the range limit of their weapons, they fired on us, and the bolts hit our force fields.

"Up you guys," I said, as the Vipeters fired at us.

"Force fields down to only fifty percent in just a few minutes," Mark said. The same message went out to the other two starships.

"What happened?" Luke asked.

"It seems like they have adjusted well to our force fields," the computer said. "I hope our weapons are just as effective."

"Computer," I said, "we don't have much time. Can you upgrade us again?"

"I am doing that right now." The computer told us that it would be a while.

"How long," I asked Mark.

"Well," Mark said, "it takes time for all the information to get computed first and then to make the new configurations for our defenses," Mark revealed.

"Stay back away from them until we get the go-ahead, but let's see how far our lazerpon torpedoes will travel to hit the Vipeters."

"We are in plenty of range for both the phasers and lazerpon torpedoes to hit their marks," Mark said. "These weapons were designed to travel as far as needed to help repel threats from both far and close to us."

"Did you hear that, guys? Let five more lazerpon torpedoes go in a large spread again, and make sure that you hit close to the middle to do the most damage from all lazerpon torpedo blasts."

"Five away," Luke yelled with enthusiasm.

"Same here," Shane said.

We shot ours right down the middle in a large spread to get the Vipeters that were right in the front. There was another large blast, and more Vipeters fell. Again the ground turned red from the heat of the blast, keeping the Vipeters from advancing forward. But the lazerpon torpedoes did less damage to the Vipeters then the last blasts had. They must have had defensive systems as well and have adjusted to our lazerpon torpedo blasts.

"Hit them with your phasers now and see if they have adjusted to that as well," Mark said.

"Fire your phasers and see how many we can get with them," I said to Luke and Shane.

We all fired our phasers at the same time, and they killed many of the Vipeters.

"Yes," I said, "the phasers are still working fine. Hit them again," I said.

The sky lit up with bright red lights as our phasers all went off at the same time, making it look like a real fight between starships from the movies we saw on Earth. We hit the Vipeters six more times with our phasers. By the time the last blasts of light from our phasers did little or no damage, we knew the Vipeters had adjusted to our phasers as well—not completely, but enough for us to drain power and make the phasers the humanoids had to defend the ground forces with not work as well. I told Luke and Shane to fire lazerpon torpedoes at the front of the Vipeters so the ground would turn red. We would keep that up until our defenses could be upgraded. One after another, we shot lazerpon torpedoes at the Vipeters, and they would kill some, but the ground turned so red that it looked like it was a lava field, and the Vipeters wouldn't cross the hot ground.

Now that we had pushed the Vipeters back to the lake area, we had at least a day and a half to get our defenses up to date with the new data that we had acquired.

"Luke, Shane, you keep watch while I fly right down the middle of the pack of Vipeters and take all that they have so our computers can adjust to everything for the large battle to come."

"Is that a good idea?" Shane asked.

"I don't know." I said. "But if things get worse for me, Mark will take over and get me out of there."

"Just be careful," my brothers told me, and I could hear the worry in their voices.

"I'll be back," I said to my brothers as I headed head-on toward the Vipeters.

I fired several lazerpon torpedoes at the frontline of the Vipeters and turned my phasers on full. I went close to the ground with force fields at 100 percent and my speed up to ten times the speed of sound. I headed right for the center of the pack. I felt a jolt—*Bam*. I screamed as I went through the pack of Vipeters, killing a lot of them, as I saw later. The force field was enlarged into a wide pass and at full strength.

"You hit them by surprise," Mark said.

"And I think that they didn't factor in the fast speed."

"Good idea, Orian, but it still hasn't proven a thing yet."

"I might have done some damage, but I still haven't gotten any new information for the computer to update our defenses," I said. "Well, Mark, I am going to hit them again but slower than last time, so we can take the full brunt of their weapons. If I get in trouble, Mark, get me home or to safety!"

"Don't worry, Orian. I will take over if things get too dangerous for us."

"Then here we go."

I headed toward the backs of the beasts at the speed of sound and fired on them with phasers as we made our pass.

I took the Vipeters from their rear, and as I approached, they fired their weapons.

"Holding," Mark said.

Our phasers killed some and at least stunned others. We took on blast after blast of lightning bolts until Mark took control and headed upward as we continued to get hit from the rear. The ship was shaking violently from side to side, even knocking me out of my seat at one point. We got out of trouble as we headed upward and away from the danger below.

"Did you get all that information, Mark?" I asked.

"Yes, Orian. We are all set, and I have sent all the information to the computer's mainframe. We should soon find out what we are up against. But Orian, we took on some damage and need to get this ship back to the shuttle bay and get it repaired or come back with another vessel."

"Ok," I said. "Did you get that Luke and Shane?"

"Yes," they said.

"You guys tell the others what has happened and our plan. Also tell them that we have bought them another day or two."

"We heard that," said Loper.

Satar and Tara said "Good job, you guys."

"I will be back soon after I replace my ship with another," I said. "Luke, Shane, you keep hitting them with lazerpon torpedoes and that will keep the ground red hot. That seems to stop them the best for now. Keep it up until nightfall, and then we will all gather back at our homes and get ready for tomorrow—according to this world's time frame.

"Shane, you and Luke keep Loper and the others up to date and try to find out how many Vipeters are left and make sure that your humanoids and the computer keeps everything up to date."

"Don't worry," Mark said. "Whatever happens to one ship or humanoid, all information gets sent back to the computer system."

I arrived at the shuttle bay and got out of the ship and looked at how dirty it was and Mark said that we had come close to the end when the force fields had failed.

"Failed?" I yelled. "Why didn't we go up sooner?"

"Well, Orian, you and I both wanted to find out how strong the new upgraded weapons were and how we can reconfigure our plasma and lazerpon torpedoes to be more effective." Mark also went on to tell me that the ship itself was designed to reflect energy, working somewhat like a force field in itself.

"But to what degree," I asked Mark.

"It's unknown, since we have never gotten to that point in our long journey as yet."

"Quit arguing," Doreen said.

"What?" I said to Amanda and Beth.

"Nothing," they said. "We just haven't seen you this concerned before."

"By the way, Doreen" asked Amanda and Beth, "how are Luke and Shane?"

I told them how brave they were and that they were still holding their ground against the ant beasts. "Didn't you guys have the viewer on in the new house?" I asked.

"Yes," they said, "and it looked like a real mess you guys got yourselves into."

I told Doreen, Amanda, and Beth that I should bring all of humanoids home and shut the portal door. But that wouldn't be the right thing to do to our new friends. We had to stop these beasts in case they entered our world and we had to fight them.

"Computer," I said, "when will everything be updated?"

"I am working on that now," said the computer. "But it will be at least ten hours before I can make the changes."

I asked Mark to come to the helm with me to keep an eye on Shane and Luke.

"You girls come too," I said. "We could use all our brainpower now, along with the computer's."

"Okay," said the girls. "On our way. But first we are going to finish what we are doing, and we will join you and Mark shortly."

When I turned on the viewer screen, I could see everything that was going on and would talk to everyone involved at the same time if I chose to, as long as the portal stayed open.

"Loper," I said.

"Yes, Orian," Loper said.

"Why don't you and your army head back to your world for now and get ready for the next round. You can bring speeders or whatever you have for transportation back with you just in case we have to evacuate that world and close the portal."

"We are just fine here," said Loper. "Satar and the others are feeding us now and will provide us with shelter until the time comes when we have to defend the line."

Mark asked Shane and Luke to put out sensors at least half a day out from the defenses just in case the Vipeters made a surprise attack in the night.

"Okay," they said. "Let us light up the ground again to hold them off until we can return to keep an eye on them."

Off went the lazerpon torpedoes, and again, the ground turned red hot, and the sand—or now actually lava—would hold them back. Then Luke and Shane went out and placed sensors in a huge line that covered all the areas where the Vipeters had been seen and beyond.

"Loper, can you come to our starship?" I asked. "A humanoid will be waiting for you at the gate and will escort you to the helm. Bring your weapon so our computer can combine our weapon strengths and give us a better chance when the main battle comes."

"On my way," Loper said. "We'll be there in just a while, Orian."

"I need you here, Loper, for now, to help us think of ways of destroying these Vipeters."

Mark told me to eat something and to calm down. "In no time, we will have the information that we need to let us win the battle that will come soon enough," he said.

I was doubtful, but still the computer or Mark hadn't been wrong yet.

"Mark, you said that the composite material of our ship took some of the blows from their weapons and didn't destroy us," I said. "Can we use some of that information to help us?"

"Yes, we will take that into consideration," both Mark and the computer replied. I kept forgetting that talking to Mark and the other humanoids, but mostly Mark, was the same as talking to the computer directly. I think that Doc set it up that way to make our journey more personal to us all.

Loper arrived and gave the humanoid his weapon.

"Thanks," I said to Loper. "You will have it back shortly."

"That's okay," Loper said. He was admiring our starship and all of the technology on it.

"Thanks, Loper. We will take you through our ship, and maybe you will do the same on your world as soon as we defeat these Vipeters or are defeated—whatever comes to first."

"We will win," Loper said in a confident voice.

"I just hope that these Vipeters don't have your weapons' signatures from the last battle that you were in."

"I didn't think about that," Loper said to Mark and me.

"Don't worry, Loper, our systems will test your weapon and see if it passes. If not, we will reconfigure your weapons to the newest configurations. I noticed that your weapon has a chip in it."

"Yes," Loper said.

"If we reconfigure your weapon, can our humanoids make chips for all your people's weapons and will they let our humanoids insert the new chips?"

"Yes," Loper said. "No problem."

What Loper didn't know was that their weapons would be ineffective against our defenses. But that was only as a safety precaution, since we had only met his people just a couple of days before, or hours depending on the new time that this planet had. I thought they seemed too eager to fight the Vipeters when the Vipeters had destroyed their planet and forced them to seek another world. But then I thought how their people must have suffered along with the rest of their old world just like us in a way. But I still wanted to be on the safe side.

Humanoid number seventy-two brought Loper's weapon back and said that it had some residue left in the memory of the fight with the Vipeters from their past war and didn't have to be reconfigured. The new chips for their weapons would be ready soon. The humanoid went on to say, "We will take them to your people in a cargo vessel, and your men can insert them today. Should only be a few hours."

"Thank you," said Loper, "and thanks for catching the potential problem before the real battle started."

"Well, Loper, we are coming up with some ideas," I said. "Hold on. Mark, can you have the ship make a satellite that we can send up into Satar's world to monitor the air and maybe make a super lazerpon torpedo that would destroy and sanitize the whole planet and kill all plant life and life as they know it, just in case?"

"I will work on that, Orian. Let's keep figuring out what we are up against," Mark said.

"Well, Mark, turning the sand into lava seemed to work, and the composite material seems to work as well. Changing the phasers worked too." I went on and said, "If we can keep on changing our weapon IDs, we should be able to keep them wondering what will be coming next." I also brought up that if we combined everything at once and kept on changing the frequency after every blast from any of our weapons, the sheer number of the blasts should confuse them. It should keep them from changing their defenses quickly.

"All that should work. Let's run through a simulation based on what we know already first, Ok?"

Loper looked at us in wonderment as the computer showed all that we had done during the day on the viewer screen, including the changes that we had made after each adjustment. The computer went on with simulations using different types of weapons and readjusting the force field and frequency of the weapons' effectiveness with different changes. We just sat back and watched the computer go to work, as it was still gathering data from the ships of both Luke and Shane. The Vipeters tried to fire upon their ships, but were falling short. This gave us some idea of their range and that they couldn't adjust their weapons to meet Shane and Luke's positions.

"Computer, do we carry a world-sanitizing weapon?"

"Yes, Orian, but this device has to be in orbit and directed at the world you wish to sanitize. It must be fired from above and spread through the whole world."

"Prepare one to go into orbit, so if worse comes to worse, we can sanitize the planet and then replenish the planet when all is said and done."

"Okay," Mark said. "You have the final word, Orian, but use this weapon as a last choice. It might even be better to fight and then close the portal if it comes to that option. Let the Vipeters move on or they will be left with nothing to eat."

"That's it, Mark! Have some satellites sent around the planet right away, and find out how they arrived on the Leamarkes' world in the first place. I will talk to Loper while you complete your mission."

"Okay," Mark said. "But do you still want me to send up a sanitizer weapon?"

"Yes, Mark. Just as a last-case scenario."

Mark took off with the new satellites to put them in orbit. He went in a larger ship with cargo bays in it to release the satellites. They were not as big as the satellites around the Earth, but they were way more advanced than the old ones but a fraction of the size.

"I don't know how we can lose now with all the new ways that we have to track them," Loper said. "If we find their ship, we can destroy them now and be rid of them forever."

"I hope so, Loper." I said.

"Luke, Shane," I said into the microphone. "How are the Vipeters now, and are they still holding their ground?"

"Yes, Orian, it looks like they're all lying down for the night."

"Leave them alone and come home for a while. Then after a few hours of rest, we will go back and hit them hard."

Luke and Shane both said there were still millions and millions of them.

"Great," I said, sadly. Thinking the worst, the computer had come up with some carpet bombs that we would use to hit them hard in the beginning.

"Orian, some of the sensors have been tripped," Luke said.

"Let's get going."

Loper, Luke, and I hopped into our starships and headed toward the battlefield. As soon as we got there, we notice that the Vipeters were only half a day away and getting closer to the main defense. Loper told his men to get ready. He told Satar and Tara that the new chips were all ready to put into the guns.

Luke, Shane, and I started hitting them with lazerpon torpedoes with alternating frequencies, which seemed to be working fine. Then we flew high above the Vipeters and dropped cluster bombs—*bam, boom*. Vipeters were flying all over the place. We kept blasting them with lazerpon torpedoes and phasers, but they still kept coming.

Loper said they were coming into range of our weapons. "Open fire," he said to his men.

All along the line, Satar and Tara's people were firing as well. The Vipeters stopped for a moment and then started forward again, firing lightning bolts, hitting our force fields with great force, but the fields held. We were holding our own against the Vipeters, but they were also doing damage to us.

The Vipeters kept coming closer to the force field line of defense, though we kept dropping them one by one. From up above, Shane, Luke, and I were blasting at the center of them with our lazerpon torpedoes and phasers, and more cluster bombs explosions were happening all over the place. There were only a few hundred thousand Vipeters left. But the force fields were failing, and so were the force fields on our starships.

"Hold the line," I said.

"Their weapons are penetrating the force field, we have to go back," Loper said.

"Okay," I said.

Loper's people were getting the full force of the Vipeters. Satar and Tara's people had to go back to the cities where the force field was still strong and not damaged. I felt sorry for Loper.

"Pull your men back to the city, Loper. The force fields are strong there, and I think the computer has reconfigured them."

We took our ships up for recharge as we watched the fighting below. Dead Vipeters piled up all over the desert floor and along the defense line. It looked like we are winning, but we were also losing men at an alarming rate.

When our starships were recharged, we reengaged into the fight and started to hit the Vipeters from behind. Satar was hitting them from the front. Then the battle came to the cities within the force fields. The force fields were starting to fail. Anomies were being killed in their homes, and the forests were being destroyed. The creatures could fight and eat at the same time.

All of a sudden, my satellites picked up motion deep in the desert. There were signatures of ships starting to take off.

"Luke," I said, "Shane, let's go get those main ships and destroy them once and for all."

"We're with you, Orian," Luke and Shane both said.

"Hold the line," I said, "while we destroy their main ships."

We quickly flew to where the ships were and open fired on their ships. The ships exploded as our lazerpon torpedoes penetrated their defenses. For some reason, the Vipeters main ship had not reconfigured its defenses, and we took them down easily. As they hit the ground, what was left exploded like a huge nuclear weapon. The blast threw our ships backward and put our ships into spins until we got straightened out.

Back to the fight we went, and it was devastation all over the place. Loper was telling everyone to head toward the portal to escape total annihilation by the Vipeters. We were still doing damage to the Vipeters. Then all of a sudden, twelve more starships entered the portal and engaged in the fight. This was too much for the Vipeters, and they turn around and headed back toward the desert. This time, it was too late. We had more firepower, and there were only a few Vipeters left. With the final blast of lazerpon torpedoes, the Vipeters were destroyed.

The Leamarkes and the Anomies were happy that their land had been saved as the Vipeters were destroyed. Loper was sad.

"I lost most of my men in the battle," he said. "A hard day for me. Can we bring in our ships to collect the bodies of the fallen?"

"Sure," Satar and Tara said.

"I see that the monkey people have been destroyed as well," Tara said. "There will have to be a lot of rebuilding in our communities again before our world can go back to normal."

"How will we dispose all these Vipeters?"

"I think if we take them out to the desert, the creatures in the desert will have a great feast."

"Luke, Shane," I said, "we're tired and will go back to our home and rest. Satar and Tara, we will come back later to help you with the bodies."

"After we collect our bodies, I would like to invite all of you to our world for some fun and excitement to get this battle off our mind," Loper said.

"Sounds good," Satar said in a sad voice, "but it will have to be in a few days after we get our dead buried as well."

"Orian, you didn't lose anyone," Loper said. "You may enter our world at any time. I'm sure all the people in our world will be happy to have you join our establishments and have some fun."

"We will come," I said, "but after we help Satar and Tara and you, Loper, gather your bodies and grieve."

"Thanks for your help."

Loper, Satar and Tara all gave thanks to their new friends.

"How about if we have a big, grand feast another day?"

"Sounds good," everybody said.

"We've got to go. See everybody later."

When we were back at the house, I asked, "Mark, did you analyze that weapon that Loper had?"

"Actually, I have a weapon," Mark said.

"How did you get that?" I asked.

"One of the lightning bolts got through the force field and hit one of Loper's men."

"That's too bad Mark. They were good people."

"Yes, they were," Mark said. "I carried the body back to Loper's men, and they told me I could keep the weapon. By the way, Orian, I told Loper that we can pass through their portals without any given notice, and he said we are welcome anytime we want to come."

"Oh my gosh, Doreen. This has been a rough two weeks for me. I hate all this fighting."

"I don't blame you," Doreen said. "You had to protect your friends."

"It's surely going to be a long time before Satar and Tara repopulate their planet," I said. "By the way, Doreen, the monkey people moved out toward the watering hole in the desert. There is lush grass there, and eventually, when they cross the desert, I'm sure the trees that the ant creatures destroyed will grow back. I left the defenses on by the desert so the Anomies and Leamarkes can live in peace for quite a while."

"Computer, how much material do we have in our cargo bay to make things we need?"

"We have enough, Orian, but if you are going to send our mining equipment away for a while with our humanoids, we should send them out and have them got two more loads in before tomorrow."

"Can you take care of this?"

The computer replied, "Yes, of course, Orian."

"Thank you, Computer," I said.

Chapter Seven

"Doreen, will you take a ride with me in the starship?"

"Well, yes, Orian. I would love to."

"Then let's get ready, and we will go through the new portal were Loper's men came from," I said. "There are a lot of friendly people there and a lot of fun things to do. So don't take too long to get ready. We probably look ugly to them anyway." I laughed. "Doreen, you look so nice."

"So do you, Orian." Doreen said.

"Why thank you, miss. I wonder if they will have dancing there."

"I don't know Orian. I guess we'll just have to check and see."

"Your starship awaits you, Doreen. Climb aboard."

We jumped in and headed toward the new portal and a new planet. When we arrived at the portal, the computer opened the gateway, and we went in slowly and carefully.

All sorts of strange-looking people were walking around. Some were flying around. I told Doreen to just wave and smile. People really didn't pay much attention to us except that the portal was rarely used.

"Doreen, where's your earpiece?"

"Oh, I must have left it at home."

"I think I have an extra one here," I said as I tossed it to Doreen.

"Thank you, Orian."

"No problem."

We looked around. There were buildings all around the place. Some were as tall as we could see. It almost looked like New York City.

"Where we can go to earn money for here?" Doreen asked me.

"Doreen, the computer system can make any kind of money that has been created. All we need is one piece, and the computer will do the rest."

We stopped the starship, got out, and walked down the street. Above us there were car-like vehicles flying and glowing signs in the air.

"It's just like looking at Las Vegas streets while lying on the ground," I said. "I hear music playing over there, Doreen. Let's go inside and see what it is like."

"This looks kind of fun," Doreen said. "There's a table over there. Let's grab it."

We had no more than sat down when in came a funny-looking waiter with four ears on top and a huge nose. He had three hands and four feet. The creature asked us what we wanted to drink.

"I don't know. What do you recommend we get?"

"I guess you are new to this place," he said. "The first drink will be on me."

"Well, thank you," I said.

Our drinks came and had straws inside the glasses. There was a yellowish green substance inside, and on the edge of the glass, there was some sort of fruit. We said thanks, and I looked at Doreen.

"You first," I said.

"Thanks, Orian," Doreen said.

"Never mind, Doreen, I will go first." I took a small sip and started coughing. "Boy, that is strong, Doreen, but it tastes pretty good."

Doreen took a small sip and said, "Just right."

There was a funny-looking machine that music was coming out of. It sounded like a honky-tonk piano, and the music really wasn't that bad.

"This is kind of nice," I told Doreen.

I waved for the waiter to come back over. He saw me, wiggled his ears, and came running over to the table.

"Yeah, how do you like your drinks?"

"A little strong," I said.

"Oh no," he said. "This is our Shirley Temple."

We laughed.

"On this planet, what do you use for money to pay for things?"

"We call them turret."

"What does it look like?" I asked.

"I will show you one," the waiter said.

The waiter showed us this piece of paper with a picture of a guy who looked like an elephant on it.

"This is five turrets," he said.

I reached into my pocket and pulled out some shiny material that I had found in the mountains.

"Is this worth anything?" I asked.

"I'll give you one hundred turrets for it."

"Okay, it's a deal," I said.

I asked the waiter about Loper.

"You helped him battle an old enemy today?" he said. "You're kidding. You fought with Loper and his men?"

"Yes," I said.

"Then the drinks are free for you all night," the waiter said.

I went on to tell the waiter that I had made a deal with Loper, and my humanoids were going to use our mining equipment to help Loper out for a week or so.

The waiter said, "You work for Loper, you make good money."

"No," I said. "Loper has lost many good men today in the battle with the ant people or Vipeters as they are called. Bravery is more than any money is worth."

"Well, you are always welcome in here anytime," the large man said. "Enjoy yourself. Tonight, everything is on us."

Every strange-looking person in the entertainment center wanted to hear about the war and about how brave Loper's men were. I went on to tell them about the battle, and then I asked if they had a way to connect my viewer screen to their systems.

"Let me see that device," the bartender said. "Yes, I think we can do it so everybody can see what happened."

"If you can," I said. "We are exhausted."

They could all watch, and we just sat there and enjoyed ourselves. The bartender also hooked viewer screen up so it would be visible to the people outdoors. Everyone looked in amazement. They were scared when they saw what we were up against. It was like watching a movie for them. The whole environment became quiet as they watched the battle unfold and saw how brave Loper's men were. They were amazed by our starships and how much damage we did to the Vipeters before the main battle by turning the ground into lava with our lazerpon torpedoes, slowing them down.

As the people watched, Doreen and I got back to our relaxation. I really didn't want to see the battle again. So Doreen and I talked, and we looked around with amazement at all of the different kinds of creatures—or people as we called them by then—came into the place. Everyone was friendly, and our earpieces worked fine, so we could communicate with everybody. Everyone came up and shook our hands. Well, some had trunks that we shook. Some creatures had ears the size of car doors. But most of the people had some sort of fingers. Some of Loper's people were in the establishment as well, but they were saddened when they heard of all of destruction.

"See how nice everyone is here, Doreen? I hope all these portals lead to friendly worlds with excitement and not war. I have liked almost everyone that I have met so far. How do you feel, Doreen?"

"Well, Orian, this is nice, but I still miss our friends on Earth and the fun times that we had both in school and on your farm with your father."

"You see, Doreen, I want to unite all these planets one by one until our world is the centerpiece for all people to gather."

"So far you are doing a good job, Orian. Let's just hope your plan works. Maybe someday, if we marry and have children, they might want to live on one of these planets. It would be nice if the portals were left open at all times."

"That is my dream, Doreen, but I am still scared to see what is behind each portal. I don't know if I should just enter each portal and see what is beyond or if I should wait for a creature to come out. Maybe I should just go to the source and then make contact. I guess I will cross that bridge when it comes."

I told the bartender or waiter that he could keep my viewer screen as a log of what Loper and his men had done for that other world and that the leaders of that world would be coming to his establishment some.

"Let's go home, Doreen," I said.

We slowly walked back to our starship. Well, it was not really a starship. It was like a flying car with defenses and computer technology. I told Doreen that we would have to come up with names for all the machines that we had. Doreen laughed.

"I'll leave it up you, Orian."

"Thanks," I said. "Doreen, you guys can help, too."

We both laughed, got into our shuttle, and went home. When we got home, Shane, Luke, Amanda, and Beth asked where we went.

"We just went out for joyride," Doreen said, "and got some fresh air."

After we got out of our car-like ship, we all went into the new house Doreen and the humanoids had built.

I looked into the girls' eyes and asked, "Why are your eyes so blue tonight?"

"What do you mean blue?" Amanda said. "I have brown eyes."

"Not tonight," I said. Shane and Luke agreed. "What have you been eating?" I asked.

"The same thing you guys have been eating," Doreen said. "The only thing that is different is that we have this world's water supply for us to drink now. The computer said it was safe to drink. Also, we have been eating some of the food that has grown already in our garden while you guys have been eating computer food."

"Maybe something in the soil or water is turning your eyes blue."

"From now on, you will be eating and drinking our new water and food as well," Amanda said.

"What about the Vipeters we brought in? Has the computer checked the meat out of these creatures? And what were the results?" I asked the computer.

"Since the creatures were eating nothing but plant life, their meat is very rich in protein."

"We have a large freezer we can put several Vipeters in. So why don't you take one of the cargo ships out?" I asked. "Luke, load up the cargo bays full of Vipeters and have the humanoids prepare them for the freezers until our cargo bay freezers are completed. The others are just about full."

"Okay, Orian," Luke said. "Shane says he will take a cargo ship to help the Anomies and Leamarkes get the bodies off their land and get them before they spoil."

"Doreen," I said. "Did you ever imagine us eating creatures like that for food?"

"I sure didn't," Doreen said. "But we will have to get used to new things on this new world and, I'm sure, on the other worlds that we will explore later."

"The livestock are ready to be put out to pasture tomorrow, and I think they will scrounge on the underbrush of the huge mushroom-like trees and bamboo droppings," Amanda said. "I sent the chickens out today, and they are already starting to lay eggs, so we will have fresh eggs in the morning. Depending how fast the cattle grow here, we will have nice T-bones again."

"Sounds good, Amanda. Thank you too, Beth, for all that you have done in the garden and with the embryos of the livestock."

As Luke and Shane went back with the cargo ships, I took a ship and flew back to help Loper gather his dead. When I arrived, I noticed that Loper and his men were stacking the bodies of their fallen men on a large pile of wood.

"We burn our bodies as a sacrifice to the source," Loper said.

"So do we," said Satar and Tara.

"What is this about the source? I don't understand," I said.

"The source in your world keeps all of our worlds alive and well," Satar said. "We have known for generations and thousands and thousands of years that the source in the middle of your world, Orian, has something to do with our water supply, soil, and just about everything around all our planets."

We stayed until nightfall. Everybody stayed quiet as the bodies burned. A large, flaming fire blazed in the middle.

Then I told Loper that Doreen and I had taken a break and gone into his world to an entertainment center. I told him I had shown the whole city how brave his men were.

"Thank you, Orian and Doreen, for doing that," Loper said. "We will have a lot to talk about for many years."

The Leamarkes and the Anomies all came back to the portal and helped with the cleanup. Now that the Leamarkes and Anomies were friends once more, they were working together as a team.

"Let's go home and tell the families that some of their husbands have died," Loper said.

As he walked away with his men, I said, "I will see you soon. Okay?"

"Yes," Loper said. "Just ask anyone where we can be found."

"Thanks again, Loper, for everything and sorry about your losses. Tell your people how brave your men were. Doreen and I will see you soon."

Shane and Luke brought back big loads of Vipeters and had the humanoids butcher the Vipeters and put them in our large freezers. Doreen and I arrived at the ship and got together with the rest of the family. We discussed what seemed to be a week or more for us, but it had only actually been a millisecond in our biological time. We still didn't know what effect this new planet would actually have on our lives.

"Computer, have you figured out a calendar year for this planet yet?" I asked.

"Still working on it, Orian. We still haven't completed even close to an orbit around the suns. With the days so long and the nights short, I can come up with some sort of watch system for you. At least you could tell what time it is during the day and the night. But as for a year, I still don't know yet, Orian, but it seems that you age much slower on this planet than on Earth."

"Boy, I hope we get in more fights like that again," Luke bellowed out.

"Why would you think that after all the people and creatures that died?" Shane asked.

"I didn't mean it that way," Luke said. "I meant to say that it was kind of fun."

"As far as our starships and humanoids are concerned, if our computer system that Doc has created hadn't been updating all the billions of years, we would not have had such luck." I said.

Mark agreed. "If our phasers and lazerpon torpedoes stayed the same strength, we would have lost the fight."

"Thank you, Mark," I said. "And thank you, Doc, for creating this wonderful ship. And thank you for letting us have such great brothers and friends."

Then Doreen and I told the rest about our trip to the world that Loper came from.

"I knew it," Beth said. "You guys were not just driving around, were you?"

"No." We laughed. We went on to tell them about all of the fun people we had met there.

"And we would go back again soon with all of you, after we get some rest and do some more work around this planet," I said. "We also need to do some more exploring of our new surroundings."

After a short rest, we got into a larger starship and flew around our surroundings, taking samples here and there from different plant life and more different soils.

"Let's go over by that waterfall," Amanda said.

"Okay," I said. "What did you see?"

"Vines and such things that reach around the waterfall and then retreat back into the waterfall."

"I don't see them," Beth said.

"They were just there," Amanda said.

I pulled up closer to the waterfall, and all of a sudden, a huge vine came around and grabbed us. It held on tightly to the ship.

"Oh my gosh," I said. "I forgot to turn on the force fields."

"Turn the force fields on," Luke yelled.

Doreen and Amanda screamed as the ship got pulled into the waterfall.

"What do we do, Mark?"

"Turn on the force fields. Then let's put voltage through the ship's hull to see if the vines will let go."

The ship was getting pulled farther and farther into the waterfall until water was all around us.

"What's happening, Mark?" I asked.

"Since the force fields were off when the vine grabbed the ship, the vines became part of our surroundings."

Then as quickly as the vine grabbed us they let go, and the ship leveled out.

"Wow, what a rush," Luke said.

"Nothing scares you, Luke, does it?"

"I guess not," Luke said.

"I was scared, and so were Amanda and Doreen," Beth said.

"Let's land the ship and see if we can get some samples of that vine creature."

We landed the ship and all got out. We turned on our force fields and went closer to the waterfall, where we could see lines under the blue—I mean dark blue—waterfall.

"This is odd," Doreen said. "The waterfall starts on top of the mountain and then falls down into the pool here. But it doesn't have a river flowing out here."

"That is odd, but nothing on this world seems to be normal."

We started to collect samples of some plant life at the base of the waterfall. As Amanda and Beth were taking samples, I looked behind the waterfall. Halfway up, I could see the vines reaching around the waterfall as if they were hugging it.

"I didn't see any river that goes behind the waterfall out to the ocean either. It is like the source at the center of our world," I said. "Rivers flow into it but not out."

"You're right," said Doreen. "Everything is stranger than it appears."

We all reached into the water, and the water felt nice and warm. There didn't seem to be fish or a strong current in the water. We all felt like jumping in to do some swimming.

"Let one of the humanoids take a swim, and if he is successful, we can all go swimming tomorrow if he says it's okay," I said.

"Yeah, let's go swimming tomorrow."

We all agreed to make it a family day and to go swimming then. We went back to the ship and headed around the mountain ranges, looking at all the different portals—twenty in all. And there was one black portal, which would make it twenty-one. That portal had an eerie sense to it. We all wondered why the other portals were shining and this one was pitch black.

"If we have any leftovers from dinner," Shane said, "we should use some of the meat as bait. We could do some fishing."

"I will join you as well," I said.

"Well, we should just all make it a big day tomorrow," Doreen said. "We will swim and fish and just have fun day for ourselves."

"Well, everyone, sounds like a plan," I said. "You guys want to take a ride around this planet? We can map some of the water depths."

"Sounds fun," said Amanda.

Off we went up over the mountain and over the ocean. We went in a straight line so we could go all way around and back. The planet was completely round. We took our time and looked at the water. The sea took on different shades of colors, anywhere from dark blue, reddish in some places, and a purple color at the other end of the ocean.

From all over the ocean, the large moons and rings like Saturn and Jupiter looked so bright in the sunlit sky. One sun of the planet seemed to hide the other sun halfway behind it. It looked like a huge heart-shaped sun. It truly was a beautiful place, and sitting over the ocean, the planet became clearer. We looked at amazement at its beauty.

"How deep is the water, Computer?"

The computer replied, "Three to four hundred feet deep is all."

So far we had a couple different deeper readings. As we flew around the ocean, we found a very shallow area, and we slowed down to take a look. Doreen asked me if we could ever build there, but I didn't know. Maybe, just maybe, we could live in another world besides ours on this planet.

"By the way, Amanda, did you see any bugs at all when you are checking out the life?"

"Why, no, I didn't," Amanda said. "How about you, Beth?"

"No, not me. Once at home tonight, we will go the down to the nursery and start hatching some insects for this planet. We'll start out with some really good bugs. I hope Doc didn't put any cockroaches in the nursery. Boy, I hate cockroaches. We will also start with some simple birds and see if they can survive on this planet."

We flew all around the new planet of ours and did not find any other landmasses or continents. I know the computer had said there weren't any, but I was just hoping for some more land. We finally got back to our landmass and flew into the valley with the rivers flowing into it. Then the clouds turned black in just a few seconds, and it started to rain. Then thunder and lightning were hitting our craft. Our force fields were holding, but this time, the lightning was all around us. We had to set our ship on auto pilot in order for us to fly to the shuttle bay.

Bam came another monstrous lighting strike and then another and another. They were finally starting to fry our force fields.

"Force fields down to forty percent," Mark said.

Then there was another bolt. This one seemed to raise the hair on our arms and heads.

"Twenty percent force fields."

Another blast of lightning hit us.

"Force fields down to five percent and falling," Mark said.

The thunder was so loud that it was actually hurting my ears. The girls jumped between the seats, and another lightning bolt hit us. This time it hit the ship, but the ship held. As we got close to the shuttle bay, we got hit by another lightning bolt. Then we bolted through the shuttle bay opening and landed. The larger ship was getting hit as well, but the computer had already made adjustments for the ship to withstand the lightning bolts.

As the lightning bolts hit the ground, we could see streaks of white light traveling through the roots of the plant life in all directions that the lights went. Once again, the mushrooms turned upside down to capture the water, as if to funnel it directly through the plant to strengthen it directly in the roots.

The sun was still as bright in the sky as when the storm had hit, but it wasn't like any other storm. The storm just appeared out of nowhere and let loose with a fury. We all liked thunderstorms, but ones that can't do damage to us or are as deadly as this storm seemed to be.

We took an elevator from the shuttle bay down to where our house was. Doreen had made the house a simple house with four bedrooms and three bathrooms, a nice living room, and a dining room and kitchen all in one. The viewer screen was in the living room, and we had electronics throughout the house. The nice garden that Amanda and Beth made was getting plenty of water from the rain because the computer was letting moisture in through the force field to be able to keep the garden watered. Everything was working fine.

"I have an idea, guys," I said.

"What is that, Orian?"

"Let's all watch a movie."

"Sure, what do you want to see?"

"We have every movie ever made," I said. "Doc saved them for us to see. You see that big book over there? It has the names of all the movies and different categories of movies. Which one of you wants to be the first one pick out a movie?"

"I do," Beth said.

"Well, what would you like to see, Beth?"

"How about *I, Robot*?"

"That is fine with me," I said. The others agreed.

Beth asked the computer, "Play the movie, *I, Robot*."

"And you humanoids watch too. See what you would have looked like if my father wasn't so smart," I said, laughing.

Everyone gathered to watch the movie except me. I wanted to go through more of Doc's logs and the starship's journey through all the billions of years of traveling through the galaxies and universes. I asked the computer to elaborate on some of the conflicts we had had during our journey and what time they were.

"This was your father's first conflict and confrontation with an alien species," the computer said. On the viewer, it showed us circling in orbit around a blue planet. I saw the mining vessels head down to the surface to gather more

ore for Doc and the computer to make new inventions and keep updating the ship as it traveled searching for a planet. When the shuttles were starting to land back at our starship, an alien starship appeared and opened fire on us.

The log showed the ship being hit hard, but the *Grant* fired back with all her fury. The *Grant* blew up several of the alien's spacecrafts and then noticed that the starship went into hyperdrive. The computer showed me more confrontations with aliens and explained why we couldn't land on their planets and try to start a new life in an earlier place and or time during our journey. There were not enough of us to put up a fight. Only a few humanoids had been made, and they were being constantly updated at the time.

The computer said to me, "Orian, we probably stopped at almost a million planets to gather material before we stopped here. We circled this planet for one year, making sure it could sustain human life and all of the wildlife and animals that Doc had collected in the nursery."

Then I thought, *What an idea. I'm going to go to the nursery to start awakening bird embryos and insects like ladybugs. Doc didn't gather any flies that I know of. And I sure hope he didn't want us to repopulate our planet with crows and other types of destructive birds and animals!* This land just couldn't handle too much wildlife because of the size and small amount of land.

I thought I would start with some embryos of seagulls, finches, and maybe some parrots and robins. The family was still watching the movie when I slipped out and went into the starship's nursery. I hoped Amanda and Beth would not be mad at me for doing some of their work. Doc had tens of thousands of each creature's embryos on hand, along with other plant life, and I would try to propagate some tomorrow. Soon Amanda and Beth came in.

"What are you doing, Orian?" they asked.

"Oh, sorry, you guys. I was just going to work on some of our plants from Earth and plant each seed in the greenhouse."

"You're taking away our jobs," said Beth and Amanda.

"Well, I enjoy farming, and I thought that I would do a little bit. Can I at least help some, Amanda?"

"Sure, Orian, we were just teasing you."

"What kind of trees do you think we should start here in the soil?"

"Any tree or flower that won't hurt native plant life."

"I would like to see some oak trees. Maybe a weeping willow or two."

"We will choose what to plant in this world," said Amanda. "Because Beth and I have been studying the plant life here on this world. But go ahead, Orian, get your birds ready. Just put them in the growing medium. That will feed your birds until they are ready to be set free."

"Thanks, Amanda and Beth. I will get that done right now. This is fun," I said. "But on the farm, how easy it was just to watch the animals do it all on their own. All we had to do was feed them."

"Ya, we remember, Orian, but you weren't much help if I remember right," Doreen said as she walked into the nursery.

"I can see I am no match . . . three to one."

We all laughed and got on with our projects. I soon had mine finished, so I decided that I would go to see how Satar and Tara and their peoples were doing. I took Mark, my humanoid, and got into one of our spacecrafts and flew into the Leamarkes' land first. Then I would go to the Anomies' homes. I landed near where Satar was and asked Satar to get into the starship because I wanted to show him something. Then we flew off to find Tara.

"Satar, Tara, I want to show you something," I said.

Off into the desert I flew. Soon, we got to the lake in the desert, which was all destroyed by the Vipeters.

"This soil is very rich here," I said. "Even the desert sand is rich in minerals. I think if we divert some of the water, we can make this land fertile and expand your territory."

"How can we do that?" Satar and Tara asked.

"Once Loper is through using our mining equipment, we can take that equipment and adapt it to dredge canals. And from there, if we put in several more canals, we would be able to flood the desert with water from the lake.

"But look over here, Satar. Just to the East is another large lake. I saw more lakes farther inland. But first, we will dig ditches and canals to get this soil damp. What do you think of my idea?"

"It sounds great," they said.

"Right now, the Leamarkes don't have a place to live and," Satar said, "we like to live high in the trees. The trees are almost gone."

"Yes, I know, Satar. That was a big disaster. Can you string your land nets from building to building in Tara's town for now?"

"Yes," Satar said. "That would be a great idea for now, if you don't mind, Tara."

"No bother at all Satar. It will take some time before the wild life and plant life gets back to normal."

"Okay then. Settled," I said. "Tomorrow your time, come and get us . . . only if it is daylight in our world. We will go and visit Loper and his family, and you can see the sights with us."

"Sounds good," The Leamarkes and Amonies agreed. "We will see you tomorrow."

"By the way, I want both of you at my place to show you a selection of trees and plant life from our planet that might grow well in your world, because someday, we might have to live in this land or one of the other worlds yet to be explored at this time. See, your world and Loper's world have met and have shared blood together for a good cause, so he is a loyal friend to you now. You are welcome to go to visit anytime that you want."

"Yes," Satar said, and Tara nodded.

I told them about my plan to unite all the planets or worlds together over the years, so everyone could leave the portals open once again.

"That would be nice of you, Orian, if you could ever make it happen."

I helped the Anomies and Leamarkes pick up what they could salvage. I worked until almost everything was done. The people on the world were still grieving the losses of their husbands and brothers and the other people who had gotten hurt in the battle.

I figured that, with all the seedlings of all our trees combined, it might just be a good combination for the world. And if we could get the desert to bloom and grow crops, we just might be able to move into the world someday. Off in the distance, I could see some of the dog-like creatures and the hammerhead shark's head animals forging around, trying to find something to eat.

"Well, Satar and Tara, I am going to head back to our world now, but I hope to see you tomorrow sometime. We will go to Loper's world on planet Saphra."

"Okay then, we will see you tomorrow," they said.

I climbed into my starship, and off I went. When I arrived back home, I thought I would take one of the speeders out for a spin around the area. I asked Luke and Shane if they wanted to join me.

"Of course we would like to come."

"Okay, brothers, grab speeders, and let's go."

We dodged in and out of plant life, driving at high speeds and just chasing each other around. We were weaving in and out of the mushroom-like plant life and through the bamboo forests. Paths between them became the pathway for our speeder racetrack. Then we decided to head to the power source.

On the way there, we spotted a very little person, and we had to stop. There were five little men—or women, we couldn't tell what they were. Their faces were all pudgy and shaped almost like potatoes and the same color. They were only about four feet tall, if even that. Their clothing looked like it was made of burlap sacks.

I heard them say, "Where did you come from? Are you dangerous?" I could tell that they were confused. We got off our speeders. We slowly walked toward them with our hands extended outward to greet them. To them, this must have seemed like an act of aggression.

They reached for some type of weapon. With our force fields on full, I reached for my weapon.

Then I said, "Put your weapons down. Luke and Shane, let's not get into a fight here." We called the people sand dwarfs, and they also put down their weapons. We proceeded to talk.

"Which portal did you come from?" I asked.

"The one just left a starship," one of the sand dwarfs said.

"My name is Orian, and these are Luke and Shane, my brothers. Who are you, and what are you called?"

"We are the sand dwarfs, and my name is Sanfe. These are my brothers," Sanfe said. "What you are doing on this planet."

"Well, Sanfe, our world has been destroyed. We were seeking a new world to live on. One day, we found this planet. I have named this planet 'Near Earth, Two' or NE-2."

"After we go to the source, may we come and talk to you at your starship?"

"Sure," I said.

"We would love that," said Shane and Luke.

We talked for a little while longer, and then off we went on our speeders again, dodging the plant life and trying to pass one another. We ran our speeders for at least another two hours before we finally headed back to our home next to the starship.

When we arrived, we told Doreen, Amanda, and Beth about the little people we had met and that they would be visiting us soon.

"And almost at any time, Doreen," I said. "Have the computer prepare something for friends to eat. Do you have some of that nice cold water that you tapped for us to drink, Doreen?"

"Well, I sure do," Doreen said. "I had the humanoids run a pipe to that stream over there and insert a water pump in the middle of the water. It is the cleanest. Plus, it all also goes through our purification process."

Not much later, Sanfe stopped in with this group of brothers. First, Sanfe was stunned by our force field.

"Open the gate, Computer," I said. "Come on in, Sanfe. Come over here and sit down. We have something for you to eat if you're hungry."

"Starving," Sanfe said. Then he said, "Let's have a feast."

As we were eating, Satar and Tara came through the gate.

"Hi, guys," I said. "Are you hungry?"

"We can have a little," Satar said. So did Tara.

I told Doreen to make a plate for each of them. I introduced Sanfe and his men to Satar and Tara.

"What world are you from, may I ask?" Satar asked.

"Our world is called Zipam. Maybe you have heard the distant legends of our planet?"

"It has been so many years," Satar said, "since our worlds talked to each other. We were friends, and names of worlds got lost over the years."

When we were all done eating, I asked Sanfe and his men if they would like to join Satar and Tara and I as we went to the nursery and planetarium to check out some plant life for Tara and Satar's destroyed world.

"I would very much like to see your starship."

"May I ask you to leave your weapons behind, Sanfe? You can leave them at the doorway of the starship and pick them up on your way out."

"Sure," Sanfe said.

I asked one the humanoids to have the weapons tested to see how much damage their weapons could do to us. "But do it discreetly," I said to humanoid 145. I asked Mark, my humanoid, to assist me with our guests.

"Yes, Orian. I would be glad to."

I told Sanfe that there were only six of us left from our world. "The humanoids were made in our image to make us feel more at home," I said.

"These are humanoids or robots?" Sanfe asked.

"Yes," I said. "But they are human and have full emotions. Most other robots or humanoids might not have that."

155

I showed the group how many millions of different species we had in our planetarium and nursery. I told them that, on our planet, we had continents separated by oceans.

"Each continent had different species of animals and plant life. On our planet, the oceans were salty and were full of fish that humans ate. I was looking at some trees here for your world, Satar. Here are some pictures of them. In the soil here, they should get to be many feet tall and reach toward the sky, just like your old trees."

After we went through the species of plant life and were talking with Sanfe, I asked him, "Am I welcome in your world? Where could I meet you?"

"Here is the key to get you through the portal, but we are not the only people who inhabit planet Zipam," he said. "We will go now. We must take this sacred water we got from the source back to our world. You are welcome anytime, Orian. Your family and you won't have a hard time finding us when you enter our world."

"Thank you, Sanfe," I said.

"We will see you soon, my friend. And nice meeting you also Satar and Tara," Sanfe said. "You're welcome to our world as well. When Orian's family enters, you should all come together."

Chapter Eight

"Tara and Satar, why don't we gather a bunch of our people and head into Loper's world. I will show you some amazement as we go through the portal, and maybe we can meet Loper's family."

"Sounds good," Satar said.

Tara also agreed that we should get Doreen, Beth, Amanda, Shane, and Luke.

"We will take one of our larger starships to be a little roomier for your people."

The Leamarkes and Amonies said that sounded like fun too. We all loaded up in a starship and went to Tara and Satar's world, where we picked up more Leamarkes and Amonies to take with us. We all took off.

Before I got to Loper's portal to planet Saphra, I said, "Watch this, you guys."

I asked Mark to turn on the cloaking device so we could go in undetected. Mark did. We entered the portal to the other world. It was still dark there. There were more lights everywhere. Car-like planes were flying all around the buildings and seemed to be stop in a high-rise parking garage. As we flew up and down the streets, we noticed all the shops to buy things in. Our computer made a lot of money to be able to buy things in the world. That sounds a little funny, us making money, but we would raise money back from our mining operations on the planet. I had let Loper take some humanoids and some mining equipment for whatever he was mining.

"Let's take a ride around the planet. What do you say, guys?"

"Sure. Anything you want to do, Orian."

"I want to see if this is a dark planet. It is colder than our planet. I wonder if gravity is stronger or if the air is hard to breathe."

We flew through the city, dodging in and out of traffic. Then we headed past the city into the country. I could see that there was light far away. I raised the starship to impulse speed and headed toward the light. We looked down and saw many homes all lit up. Little cities seemed to pop up everywhere. Finally, we got to the other side of the planet, and there was a sun. It was not very large, no matter how fast the planet orbited around its axis, or if the planet even rotated. All of it must have had gravity that strong.

We headed back toward the main city at eight times the speed of sound. We saw one city ahead of us, and we thought we would stop and check it out. We pulled in toward the city and uncloaked our starship. As soon as we landed in the city, we saw what looked like an entertainment site. We decided to go in and get drinks. We were hoping that they would have ice cream sundaes, but we were only dreaming.

We started walking down the path to the building and were ready to enter the building, when we saw what looked like Loper's kind of people. I stopped them and wanted to know who they were. They had their weapons drawn, but we had our force fields on, though we were worried about Tara and Satar; they did not have force field belts.

"You know Loper?" we asked them.

"Why, yes. He is our president," they said.

"Well," I said, "Loper, is a very close friend of mine; we just went through a large battle. Was that you?"

The men said, "Yes, that was us. We are sorry about. And the people that you have lost."

"Where can I meet Loper?" I asked.

"Let's get on the radio and contact Loper. He can show you around the place."

We went inside with our new escorts. They were still looking at us kind of funny.

I looked them in the eyes and said, "I'm going to get something to drink, you guys. What would you recommend?" I asked.

In a stern voice, they said, "The isotopes are the best price."

"Thirteen isotopes all around."

"How are you planning to pay for all those?" the slammers asked.

"With this," I said as I laid a pile of cash down on the table.

"Where did you get all that money?"

"Hey, man, what's your problem?"

We were just about ready to break out into a fight when Loper walked in.

"Stop it, you guys," Loper said. The slammers shut up.

"Hi there, Loper," I said to him. "What is this attitude that your men have toward us?"

"You see," Loper said, "we own this half of the planet, and we hire people from all the cities to work and mine. Some of my guys think they're really tough."

Loper told the slammers in the bar that they were lucky that they did not draw their weapons. He told them our weapons were much more superior.

"They would've annihilated you in an instant," he said. "We don't want that, do we, boys?"

"No Sir, Mr. Loper."

"These are my friends, whom I have had the privileged be in battle with, the ones that everyone is talking about. This is Orian, Doreen, Shane, Luke, Amanda, Beth, Satar, and his friends called the Leamarkes and Tara and his friends the Amonies."

"Loper," I asked. "is this a dark planet where the sun barely shines?"

"No, this is our cold season right now. When it becomes summer, it stays light for many days. Time is similar to your planet in some ways. So on one half of the planet, it is planting season. The second half of the year is our growing season for food."

"Okay, I understand Loper. Can your men learn how to drive the mining machines?"

"Yes. Why would you ask?"

"Because I was thinking, if you need them that badly, you can have the mining machines and send the humanoids back. What kind of mining operation do you have? What is the purpose of your mines?"

"This is how we create power on this planet, by mining our natural resources."

"We did that on Earth," I told Loper, "until it ruined the environment and caused severe global warming. The bad climates that followed us took a toll on the people all over the globe.

"Loper," I continued, "we all thought that we would come here and surprise you. I guess we got the surprise. In the city by the portal, all the people were very friendly. As we got deeper into the country, it seemed that the people got less friendly. Is it always this way, Loper?"

"No," Loper said. "There is a bad bunch in every group of people."

Satar agreed.

"Tara, Loper," I said, "we met some people from that third portal, and we have been invited in. I thought, the next time we all get together, you could join us and meet the new people on the planet Zipam. The people are called sand dwarfs, and they really seemed to be a nice race of people."

"Those drinks hit the spot. They are very sweet."

"Shall we have another?"

"Fill them up," Loper said.

Another round of drinks came to all of us. This tavern was mostly made up of Loper's kind of people.

"What is your people's race again, Loper? I forgot."

"Our real names are Celanas. Thank you. Thank you for the mining equipment, Orian. I will pay you dearly, so you'll have plenty of money to spend on our planet."

"Can you make more machinery?" Loper asked. "Yes, we can, but you will have to bring the ore to us. Any material—rocks, sand, or anything you can load into the cargo ships. I will need plenty of material for our ship's computer to create more machinery for you. So when you get a chance to have a big load, you can dump it next to our force fields. Just unload it there or ask one of our humanoids to let you in to dump it in our material bays.

"We will go now, Loper," I continued, "and I will take my friends back home. We will meet again. Please bring us material so that we can work with the builder to build your new mine machinery."

Loper told one of his boys to give us a large sum of money.

"This is for your machinery," Loper said. "There will more when you have more mining machinery ready for us. Thank you."

"Yes, you are welcome," I said.

We returned to our starship. When we left, I put on the cloaking device. You should have seen the look on Loper's face as we disappeared right in front of his eyes and took off. We did, however, make one more stop: the entertainment center that Doreen and I had gone to earlier.

"Now, this looks like a nice place," Satar said.

"It is," I said. "Come on, let's go. Hey there, my friend," I said to the four-legged bartender.

"I see that you're back, and you have brought more friends."

"Not too busy for you . . . ?" I asked.

"Nah, you want the same as you had before?" "Yes I do . . ." I said, "And a round for everyone. I am big spender today. Just got paid by Loper for mining equipment that I sold them. As we speak, my humanoids are on their way back home."

"Prettier women," the bartender said, "but I remember this beauty; Doreen is your name, isn't it?"

"Why yes, it is," Doreen said. "You remembered."

"Why yes, I did. I can never forget a pretty gal."

"By the way, guys," I said, "the bartender's name is Lepkwod. Hey, Lepkwod."

"Yes, Orian?"

"What is the whole deal behind Loper's operation?"

"Well," Lepkwod said, "his people, the Celanas . . . when making this planet a new place to live, they immediately started to take over. We do have a central government here in our world, but the Celanas have taken over power of almost all of the government. They own most of the businesses, you see—except mine of course." But Lepkwod went on to say that the Celanas had been good to the people. "Most of the time, he pays a good wage to working-class mining operators. But in other endeavors, he treats his people poorly."

"I get the picture now, Lepkwod. When I unite all these worlds through these portals, everyone will be treated equal, and we will help each other out."

"You think that could ever happen?" Lepkwod asked.

"Sure," said Orian. "Anything is possible."

"When Orian makes up his mind, Lepkwod," Doreen said, "things get done."

"Lepkwod, you should take your starship, to our farm, not the source, and come visit us sometime. We will serve you instead of you serving us."

"That would be fun," Lepkwod said.

"I would do that very quickly. In the meantime, Lepkwod, keep your ears and eyes open."

Satar and I looked at Tara and asked, "What do you think about Loper?"

"He seems to be a stand-up kind of guy, but it's hard to tell sometimes when you don't really know all the facts: what is going on, how he may be earning a big salary on the backs of other creatures that live on this planet. I will have to check on this a little more."

We pondered it all the way back to Satar and Tara's world.

"I thought we should sit down with their people, have them discuss what is going on in the other worlds where Loper lives, how we got treated as soon as we landed just trying to go into an establishment to get a soft drink."

After dropping off the Leamarkes and Anomies, Doreen and I and the rest all headed for home. We decided that we should go through the ship's logs and see if any of the other probes we had sent out had sent back any information.

"I just hope I'm doing the right thing by building more mining equipment for Loper and his gang," I said. "So far, he's done no wrong. He has helped us fight a battle where he lost many good men and did help us get out of a bad situation. He has been very cordial to us in every way. I will still send my thanks to Loper for all his help in our time of need.

"Mark," I said, "tell the systems director to make four more big mining ships for Loper and his people. Keep one for us and the humanoids coming back home. They are through the portal on the way back to base."

The computer felt that the humanoids were working very hard and were not able to rest and recharge.

"If this is so," I said, "Loper might treat his people and workers the same. This does disturb me, Mark. When the humanoids arrive, make sure they get cleaned up and get plenty of recharge time. What has the computer found out on the status of the weapons that the sand dwarf people had?"

"We did the analysis," the computer replied. "They are not very sophisticated weapons. Their design is more to stun prey than to kill prey."

"That is good to know, Mark. You have been good humanoid to me. I respect all your advice. Computer, what about those lightning strikes we had yesterday? Is there any way that you can protect us further from those dangerous storms?"

"Yes, Orian," the computer said. "I have already made changes to our force fields. We will need more ore soon, so we can program the system and make more machinery and humanoids."

"Hold off on the humanoids, computer," I said. "We have enough for now. Have some of the humanoids make some pods so we can allow many to rest and recharge. We will need them again for either a fight or to build a bigger community."

I went back down to the house and sat in front of our viewer screen. I asked the computer to put on a good science fiction movie. The computer selected *Avatar*, and we all sat down together and watched.

As we watched the movie, I thought, *Hmmmm, the Celanas look kind of like the avatars. Except the Celanas are green, and the avatars are blue. The Celanas don't fly on dragons either!* But the creatures in that movie could be compared somehow to some in the Leamarkes' world. We were humans trying to colonize this small piece of land. We were not trying to destroy resources and interfere with the other people that we had met.

We had to find a way to have more time for ourselves and start doing fun things with our friends, even the humanoids. We planned to go swimming and fishing, and that was the first thing we would do when we woke up the next morning. We had left over ant creatures that we had for dinner, and Luke saved treats for the fish we all planned on catching. We talked about a nice swim and fishing while watching the movie and got excited. I knew we couldn't go out in the ocean fishing yet, because of the large creatures, but in time, I would have the computer make a large ship. At the very least, it would be used to go fishing out in the ocean. I already had some designs made for how I wanted my fishing vessel made.

We had all been trying to keep our eyes open during the movie, but Beth and Amanda had already dozed off. I put a blanket over them. I told Doreen that I was going to hit the sack too. Doreen, Shane, and Luke said they were right behind me.

"I wish that the nights were longer so I could sleep longer, but I can always shut the viewers and keep the room dark," I said. "I think that's what I'm going to do tomorrow: sleep in."

Chapter Nine

The next morning, we were all refreshed. We got up and prepared to go fishing and swimming Amanda, Beth, and Doreen were going to hit the swimming hole while Shane, Luke, and I were heading to the mouth of the river to try to catch some fish. Each of us would pack a lunch and take speeders to the areas that we would be going too. The waterfall was close to where we would be. Mark and a couple other humanoids were with us to check out the water and to help us if we caught a big fish or something to eat for dinner.

The gals went to the watering hole, and a humanoid jumped in and found that the water was just right. There were no whirlpools, which we thought might be there. The water just disappeared into the small pond. Doreen went in first and then Amanda and finally Beth.

"Not too bad," they said. "The water is just like bath water."

They were swimming around, spraying each other when one of the vines grabbed Doreen and pulled her up into the air and into the waterfall. As she disappeared, the rest yelled "Doreen!" but only heard laughing from behind the falls. Then a vine-like hand came out and grabbed Beth, leaving Amanda on the shore screaming. Then, as quickly as they had been grabbed, they were thrown back into the pond with a big splash. The vines seemed to wave at us all and were just playing with us, taking the gals and throwing them high into the falls and then dropping them into the pond. It was just like cliff diving back home. The girls were having a blast. We were playing with the unknown.

Mark and I, along with Shane and Luke, left and arrived at the fishing spot. Close to a deep part of the slowly running river, we baited our hooks with Vipeter meat and tossed our lines into the river.

"Shall we use a bobber?" Luke asked me.

"Not yet," I said. "Let the bait get to the bottom of the stream first. Then we will try a bobber."

We sat on the riverbank, just enjoying the sun and watching our poles. We jerked the bait now and then to tease any fish that might be in the river. We tried everything but held still with our mouths open while we waited to get a nibble or two.

Then Shane gave his pole to Mark and went out to the shore. As he was picking up shells as big as a platter, he scooped out a snail-like animal that was in the shell. He brought it to us and grabbed his pole from Mark. He reeled it in and took off his meat bait. He put on the snail and threw the line back into the water. *Bam*—Shane's pole bent straight down and almost pulled Shane into the river. Mark held onto Shane as he fought a creature on the end of the line. This bright red fish thing jumped high into the air and back down into the water.

We watched as Shane fought the monster fish. Luke and I reeled in our lines, took off the bait, and tried to help Shane. Shane fought and fought with the fish until it finally got tired and slowly came close to the bank of the river.

"How are we going to get this fish onto the shore, Mark?"

"With the gaff that we have with us, Shane."

"Nice going," I said.

Mark hooked the beast with the gaff and pulled it onto the shore. It was huge and had soft fins that ran all the way down its back. It had leg-like fins on its side and the sharpest teeth that I had ever seen. At last, it was ours.

"Got one," we yelled out to the girls. "Doreen, you have some work to do now. We can try him out for dinner tonight."

"No way," Doreen said. "You caught him, you gut him. Then I will fry him."

"I'll do it," Luke said.

"No," said Mark. "This is Shane's fish, and fishermen always have to clean their own fish."

"This is so large that we will have a hard time getting it back to the ship."

"I'll gut it now," said Shane.

He stabbed his knife into the belly of the fish, and the fish started flopping all around. Shane stabbed it again and opened the belly even more until the fish stopped flopping around. Mark took his phaser and cut the fish's head off and threw it back into the river. Then all of a sudden, smaller fish were cleaning the carcass right to the bone.

"Now that is bait," I said. We decided to keep some of the carcass as bait.

"As soon as we get into the ship, have it processed and checked out for eating, then frozen. Except for what we are eating for tonight."

"That was fun," we all said. "Mark, can you take our poles and catch of the day back to the ship? I will go with Shane over to the girls and try vine jumping to get this fish smell off of us."

"Okay," Mark said. "But keep your force field belts on, even in the water. It just might save your life."

"Yes," we said.

Then off we went to go swimming with the girls. We smelled like dead dogs. When we got to the girls, the vines grabbed all three of us and took us up high into the mountains and dangled us around for a while. Then they dropped us into the pond.

"What a rush," Luke said.

"I thought that my stomach would go up out of my mouth," I said.

"Fun, wasn't it?" asked Doreen.

"You bet. How do you get them to play with you?" I asked Doreen.

"Just reach around the back and grab the base of the vine. It will grab you. I think that the vines really like it."

So I grabbed the back of a vine, and up I went right through the center of the waterfall. It was hard to breathe at times. Then the vine would hold me over the pond and drop me.

"Oh shoot, this is way too high," I yelled as I went down toward the bottom of the pond. I went way under and had to swim really hard to get back to the top of the water.

"I am getting a little cold after being in the water so long."

"Yeah, we have had enough fun too," said the boys.

We packed up our belongings, hopped on the speeders, and headed back to the ship, racing each other through the underbrush and just missing the large mushroom plants and bamboo trees. It seemed like only a few minutes before we reached home. It was at least an hour away on speeders, but we were just having fun.

We put our things away, and we all took fresh showers while Mark got the results from the fish that Shane caught.

"Nice and tender," he said. "Should taste like cod if it's prepared right."

"I will cook it right, Mark," said Doreen. "I love to cook, and we have had the computer do all of our cooking lately. Sooo, I will prepare the meal while you guys get what you have planned for the rest of the day done."

I told Doreen that I was going to go and see if the insects I had were ready to let go. The same with the birds. Amanda and Beth said that they would come as well, so we all went into the nursery and planetarium together, except for Shane and Luke. Shane was busy bragging about his catch of his lifetime.

"Look at all those ladybugs, Amanda."

"Millions of them. Let me take a few handfuls to put in the cornfields. I even have ladybug food so they don't get starved with any bugs to eat," I said. "Look at those seagulls. Put some of these birds and insects in this cage, and we will take them all outside and let them loose. The hummingbirds will love the nectar that the mushroom vines on them with all that fruit. And we will let loose some flies as well to help with the compost piles. Got everything, you guys?"

"Yes," Beth said. "I have some small pigs and three cows on my auto cart to let loose in the barnyard."

"Okay then, let's go and start life on this planet."

We brought our cargo outside, and then I gathered everyone and said, "Well, let's start creating a new Earth.

But first, let me ask Satar to leave the portal door open so some of our birds and bugs can survive on their planet too and be on ours to do some good as well. Let's do the birds first."

Beth opened the cage door, and off flew the seagulls. They automatically headed for the water edges. Then the parrots, beautiful birds, were flying all over. We let the flies loose outside the force field so they couldn't get into our food right away. Then we let the ladybugs loose all around our plants, and they flew off into the mushroom trees. They were landing all over our arms. Then we let the hummingbirds loose while Amanda put up hummingbird feeders. We let over five hundred of them loose and still had thousands of them left in the breeding pens.

The plant life seemed to start to glow a bit as birds landed on them. The hummingbirds started on the flowers full of nectar. Then they started pollinating the mushroom fruit vines without the strong winds and rain.

After we sent new life on its way in this new world, we planned to plant some of our grasses and trees in the near future especially for the cattle and corn for the hogs.

"Boy, this was a fun day, guys, and it felt good after all the bad days that we have had with all the fighting and death."

Doreen cooked the fish, and we sat down for some French fries and freshly fried fish. It was delicious. We had homemade bread and chocolate cake afterward.

"I am stuffed," I said.

"So am I," said Luke and Shane.

"Thank you, Doreen, for the beautiful dinner."

"You're welcome, you guys."

"Tomorrow, we will go to the sand dwarfs' planet and see what their world is like."

"Okay, Orian."

We all sat down and listened to Doc tell us through the viewer screen at home about our journeys and what he expected us to do. We watched as we ate. One time, we had lost part of our wing in a firefight, but it was repaired quickly, and we got the hell out of there fast.

"Well, guys, I am going to close my viewers and windows and get going to bed," I said. "Get a good night sleep."

"I will be going to bed soon, too," Doreen said.

"Same here," the rest said.

Soon the house was quiet except for the birds chirping around their feeding grounds where we had plenty of bird seed.

"Good night all."

"Good night, Orian."

"Boy, did I sleep in. I wonder what time it is in the sand dwarfs world?"

"Yes, get up now and see if Luke, Shane, and Amanda, Doreen, and Beth are up yet. Today is the day we get to meet the sand people. We are going to a different world."

I walked out to the kitchen, and Doreen was up and getting a glass of milk.

"Can I join you, Doreen?" I asked.

"You know better than that, Orian."

"Where are Amanda and Beth?" I asked.

"Still sleeping. We had a fun day yesterday. We must have really tired ourselves out yesterday, swimming and catching that big fish then going on the speeders through all the vines and plant life."

"Yes, it was a fun day, Doreen—if we can even call it a day. It is still light out. I think I'm getting used to the longer days. Maybe eventually, we will be able to stay up the full six days before nightfall," I said, laughing. "I will go out to the chicken pen to grab some eggs for breakfast."

"Can the computer make you some bacon to go along with our eggs?"

"Sure," I said. "The smell of the fresh-cooked breakfast should wake up the rest of the gang."

I went out to the chicken pen, and sure enough, there were over fifteen eggs in there, so I gathered the eggs and brought them into the house.

"Look at all these eggs, Doreen. Why don't we scramble all the eggs for one large meal?"

"Fine," said Doreen. "Start cracking the eggs, and here's the whisk. You can at least do that, can't you, Orian?"

"Yes, I can handle that."

I put all the eggs in one large bowl and started scrambling them.

"You have to add some milk to the eggs," Doreen said. "Boy, I can't wait until we get real milk from a cow."

"Won't that be nice, Doreen?"

"Yes," Doreen said. "Okay, give me the scrambled eggs, Orian."

"Here you go, Doreen."

Doreen started cooking breakfast.

"Boy does that smell good," I said. "And sure enough, here comes the rest of the gang."

"What smells so good?" Luke asked.

"Well, we have fresh eggs from the chicken pen, so we are having bacon, scrambled eggs, and homemade bread toast."

"After we eat, we are going to go see the dwarf people and talk to Sanfe."

"Yes," Shane said.

"Let's make today a fun day too. At least, I hope it will be," I said.

"That was a good meal, Doreen."

Doreen said, "You can thank Orian as well. He went out to the chicken pen, got the eggs, and scrambled them."

"Well, thanks, big brother. About time you pulled your weight."

"Hold on, Luke," I said. "You're going to get a head rub if you keep that up."

We all laughed.

"How shall we approach the sand people today? Shall we just go through the portal? Sanfe said it was okay."

"Yes, I think so," Doreen said. "What do you think, Mark?"

He agreed. "It should be okay."

"Have you checked all the weapons, Mark?"

"Yes, I have, Orian. And I think we should take the shuttle in. I think we should go in cloaked once more, until we see what kind of land this is."

"I agree, Mark, even though the dwarf people and Sanfe seemed nice enough. I think we should enter on the safe side," I said. "Well, everybody, let's get loaded into the starship, and let's take at least five humanoids with us to guard the ship while we are at the dwarf people's house."

Out of the shuttle bay we went, and in no time, we were in front of the portal.

"Put us in cloaked mode, Mark."

"Will do," Mark said.

Into the portal we went. It must have just been sunrise there. The sky was orange in color, and it was kind of a desert world. We saw tiny huts spread all over the desert with little gardens around each one. That must be how they fed each other. We stayed cloaked and flew above the planet to take a survey of our surroundings. We notice some nearby towns that had a lot of activity going on, like different spaceships landing on space pads. There were weird-looking people just like in Loper's world. Spaceships were coming and going, heading off into the galaxy. The planet had one sun along with three moons. Their planet was hotter and drier than the previous two worlds we had visited.

We stayed cloaked until we flew back to the portal door. Then we uncloaked ourselves. The sand dwarfs ran around us as if they were scared of us. Then we saw the home I believed was Sanfe's where he stood with his reddish cloak. They all looked the same, but we probably looked the same to them.

We landed our starship close to where Sanfe was and got out. I called out Sanfe's name.

"Oh yes, Orian. Welcome to planet Zipam."

I thanked Sanfe, and he asked me if I wanted something to drink.

"Sure," I said.

"Orian, you are all welcome here."

I asked Mark to take the first drink.

"I will test it," said Mark. "This is fine water."

We all partook of the drinking water. Sanfe and his people, the sand dwarfs, gathered all around our spacecraft and were just as interested in us as we were in them. I told Sanfe that we had seen a town on the way in, and I asked where all the ships came from.

"All over the galaxy," Sanfe said. "They come here for recreation and fun and to do business. Our precious resources are fuel for their starships. They come to eat and get supplies. You see, Orian, our whole planet is not a desert. There are people like us that do nothing but farm for the visitors that come."

All of a sudden, a spacecraft appeared and started to fire upon our position.

"Quick. Into the starship," I said. "Let's defend ourselves."

We hurried up into the air and engaged the ship. We rocked as we got hit by one of their torpedoes. It didn't do much damage though.

"Lock on the target and hit them with a lazerpon torpedo," I said. "Right on, Luke. Fire."

Their ship took a large hit and went spinning off into the distance. But the ship was able to regain control and come back around and engage us again.

As we avoided a few well-aimed shots to our ship, Mark said, "Don't worry, Orian, they are no match for us, and they will be destroyed if we fire upon them again."

I turned the ship around and hovered there, waiting for the ship to attack. *Bam, bam* came two hits to our force field. But we were still there. Another two hits . . . and nothing. So I put the phasers at 20 percent and fired back, more to concern them than to destroy them. It seemed to work. Even with our phasers set at only 20 percent, we still outmatched them in a fight. Soon the ship took off toward the city, limping along nice and easy as smoke came out of one of its main engines.

"Let's follow them," I said.

"No," said Doreen. "If you want to fight, you go ahead. But without us."

"Same here," said Beth and Amanda.

"I am with you, Orian," Luke bellowed. "Let's get them."

"Okay," I said, "but I am coming back without you."

As the threat diminished, we landed again and asked Sanfe if all the newcomers got this kind of treatment.

"Yes, I am afraid they do," said Sanfe. His people would leave us alone, but they tried to steal other spaceships to be able to sell them on the open market in different galaxies.

What a world, I thought to myself.

"I don't like it here," Doreen said. "After we are through dining with Sanfe and his people, let's go home Orian."

"I am with you, Doreen," Beth and Shane said.

"I will come back later with Mark and some other humanoids to check this place out," I said.

"Thanks, Sanfe," we said as we got into our spacecraft.

Then we left through the portal to come back another time, but before I left, I told Sanfe that we would come back and fight the people if they wanted a good fight on their hands.

"What do you think, gals?" I asked. "Do you mind if we drop you off and then come back?"

"That is fine with me," Doreen said. "I really don't want to get in any fights today. And Orian, you should be careful too. Be very careful."

I asked Sanfe if we could come back. He said sure, but Sanfe said not to let those little skirmishes bother us.

"It does bother us," Luke said.

"And it bothers me too," I said.

"Sanfe, do you want to ride with us while we take the girls home?"

"Sure," he said. "I have never have ridden in such a nice ship before."

"Come on, Sanfe, and bring a few of your friends."

"Okay," he said.

They all climbed in, and off we went back to our spaceship to drop the girls off. We soon arrived at our home. I told Shane to stay with the girls while I had Luke grab some humanoids and another ship. I wanted to meet at Satar's home, which was now in the city with Tara's people, the Amonies. I told Sanfe that I had some new friends that I would like him to meet.

Then away we went. As soon we entered through the portal of the Leamarkes and the Amonies' world, I flew to our old base downtown in the Amonies' villa, as I called it now. Looking back, the war that had just happened a week before seemed to have happened years before.

Down came the people to greet us. Satar and Tara had been sitting down for their morning cup of . . . well they called it coffee, but I called it mud. It was so strong-tasting, and it was made out of the stems of multar plants that were grown there. They were a bean-like plant with the taste of chicory.

"Satar and Tara," I said, "I would like you to meet a few friends of mine, the sand dwarfs from another portal to a planet called Zipam."

"Hello and welcome," they said to Sanfe and his friends."

"Boy, what happened here?" asked Sanfe.

"That's what is left after the war with the Vipeters," I explained.

"And you thought what you saw on my world was bad? Oh no. This is much more destructive," Sanfe said. "We don't have problems with the people that come to our planet. There is mostly fighting amongst the people that come to visit for food and supplies."

Chapter Ten

"Sanfe, why don't you and your sand people climb aboard my starship. Satar, why don't you and some of your people join us?" Before I finished, in swooped Luke. "What took you so long, Luke?" I asked.

"I helped calm the girls down before I came here. They were a little upset and felt in danger during the brief attack."

"How many humanoids did you bring?" I asked Luke.

"Just six," Luke said.

"Tara, why don't you and some are your people ride with Luke and fly back to planet Zipam?"

"Okay."

We all agreed.

"Then let's make this another fun day and see how many new people we can meet."

"Sanfe, what do you use for money on your planet?"

"Zarra," Sanfe said.

"And Sanfe, do we have anything we can sell so we can have some zarra?"

"Well, let's see, Orian. My wife could use one of those humanoids to help in the field."

"How much are you willing to pay for a humanoid?" I asked.

"One thousand zarra," Sanfe said.

I radioed back to the computer: "Please make one humanoid for Sanfe, one that has a self-train mode and no knowledge of our ship or emotions."

"That will be an easy one to make," the computer replied.

"How long before you can have one ready, Computer?"

Mark looked at me and said, "Probably within a few hours or so."

"Is that okay with you, Sanfe?" I asked.

"Yes, completely fine," Sanfe said.

"How far will a thousand zarra get us?" I asked.

"That should last you quite a while if you don't buy something expensive from us or from the other people that visit our planet. And also, Orian, be careful what you buy. Sometimes, they make it work for just a little bit, and then it breaks down on you."

"I will keep that mind, Sanfe. Can I bring you back the humanoid later when it is ready?"

"Yes, that would be fine," Sanfe said.

"Computer," I said, "make that two humanoids, and also make the humanoids the size of our humanoids with good strength. How does that sound, Sanfe?"

"That's all you have to do?"

"Not quite, Sanfe. It takes a while to be able to have the knowledge to create these humanoids and design them like you need, Sanfe."

"We don't use money on our planet," said Satar. "We barter for everything we get."

"That is a good way of doing things. That way, nobody seems to be richer than the other person."

"Luke, will you return later to get the humanoids for Sanfe? But first, we will meet some people and have some fun. Be careful, Luke, you are more hot-tempered than I am, so don't provoke any fights with your wisecracks."

"Okay, big brother," Luke said. "I will be good."

When we got to Sanfe's portal, Mark said, "Open portal." and through the portal we went.

"Which city do we go to?" I asked Sanfe.

"Keep going straight, Orian. You can't miss it. Now maybe you can speed."

I laughed.

"This is just a walk compared to what these babies can do."

With our force fields on high, we entered a city where there were spacecrafts of all different shapes, sizes, and colors. Some were battered and scarred from battles. Creatures of all kinds were walking the streets, and vendors and people were selling things that they had made. The streets were filled with vast amounts of food supplies. As I looked up to the left, I saw a big refueling depot.

"What do most of the ships use for fuel?" I asked.

"They use anything from nuclear power to a fossil fuel gas. We a have very limited supply of those, and they are usually much slower ships. What do you use for propulsion?" Sanfe asked.

"We use what is called a Taperian force erupter. It is a design that our late father constructed for long space travel. Actually, we store energy, and our erupter creates more power than it uses. So we can reenergize the force fields and our weapon systems faster as well."

"Park your ships over there," Sanfe said.

Away we went to the shuttle and starship parking area. There, we were met by several creatures that asked what they could do for us.

"Hey, Sanfe, I see that you come to visit. Who are your slaves?" they asked.

"No, not slaves," Sanfe said. "These are our new friends. They are from the land of the source."

"Alright," said the creature that looked like a lion. It stood on two feet but had hands with only three fingers on them. He said his name was Altria and was asking us all sorts of questions.

"We are fine for now," I said. I had two humanoids by my side to stand guard at each ship. We were proud of our gleaming spacecraft, which was looking nice and shiny. Ours was spectacular compared to the rest of the ships that we had seen here so far.

"Let's go to the Linney Club, and we can grab something to eat. But like I said, don't provoke anyone in there. There are several fights in this part of our world every day."

"We won't, I promise you, Sanfe."

"Good, then everything is on me today."

As we walked into the establishment, everyone looked at us as if we were the aliens, and in a way, they were right. We were new to the star system, and I didn't think that anyone there had ever been to Earth, let alone had ever seen a human before. As I walked in, one fly-like alien bumped into me and asked me if there was a problem and told me to apologize, but I refused to apologize and just told him that I wasn't trying to bump into him.

"Look out, Orian," Sanfe said. "They are a mean bunch of people."

"I'm okay" I said. "Besides, they only brushed against my force field, and I didn't even feel it."

Then I told everyone, even the humanoids, to reduce the shields to only one inch away so we wouldn't bump into anyone again. We did, but we did keep our shields at full strength. Then there was another alien that looked like a human but with three ears and four eyes.

"What are you looking at?" Luke asked.

"I guess nothing," it said.

"What do you mean by that?" Luke asked.

"Nothing," the alien said.

"What is your problem?" Luke asked, in a smart voice.

"Luke," I said. "Cool it."

Then the alien and some of his friends came over and threw a glass of some kind of drink at Luke. It did not penetrate his field, but it looked like it did. I stood up and told them to leave us alone while we did business there. Then one of them took out his weapon and shot at me. My force field took the whole force.

I looked at him and said, "Is that all that you got, bub? No? It is my turn."

I hit him with just my force field. When my hand reached within an inch of his body, he went flying backwards.

"Who else wants a piece of us?" I asked.

"We're cool. We just wanted to see what you are made of." he said. "Where do you hail from?"

"We were from a star system called the Milky Way. Our home planet was called Earth."

"Never heard of that star system," the aliens replied.

"Yes, it is many light-years away, and we have just found this destination. Well, Sanfe, we better be off," I said.

"Yes," Satar and Tara agreed. "Let's go and promise each other to meet again."

"By the way, Sanfe, I believe that your humanoids are ready, so come by and get them anytime you want, or we could bring them by. Whichever comes first."

When we reached the outside, we saw a commotion over by our ships. The humanoids were in a gun battle with some aliens that had just gotten off another ship nearby. It looked like they were trying to steal something from our ship, but the humanoids had to defend themselves. So far, there were many aliens lying on the ground hurt because, the humanoids had their phasers on stun as commanded by Mark.

I asked Mark to have them stop firing, and they did. But the aliens kept on firing, even with no harm coming to them. Soon the fighting stopped as Sanfe was seen walking back with us to our ships.

"Are these creatures with you?" asked one of the aliens.

"Yes," said Sanfe.

"We just wanted to borrow some fuel cells from them, and they opened fire on us."

"That is untrue," I said.

"You calling me a liar?" he asked.

"No, but let's just all see. Open hologram viewer," I told Mark.

He did, and a huge screen appeared.

"Play back the last ten minutes of log," I said.

Mark played back the log, and sure enough, the aliens got out and started toward our ships. The humanoids had given them every opportunity to get back, and they had opened fired on our humanoids. Then the humanoids finally fired back in self-defense. I asked the aliens if they would like to change their stories and told them that our humanoids would have their guns off stun the next time they wanted to fight us.

"No, that is okay," they said, and they picked up their men and headed off to the tavern.

"Smart move," Sanfe said.

"Yes, that was kind of cleaver wasn't it?" I said, laughing. I asked everyone to get into the ships and get ready for takeoff.

We all climbed in and took off toward Sanfe's hut. I told them that I thought it was a rough planet. Not all of the time would we be so lucky. Sanfe agreed and said that, as quickly as an argument started, it ended and usually with only a few deaths.

"But you are a strong race and much more advanced than the others that come to our planet."

"We are strong in technology."

Luke and I laughed.

"If only they knew the real technology of our planet." When it all ended on earth, they would have laughed us off the streets. Maybe our old handguns of the past world would have done some harm, but I don't think they would have done much.

We arrived at Sanfe's hut and dropped him and his men off. Then we said our good-byes and told him that we hoped that we hadn't caused him any trouble with the scene we had created.

"Just another day on our world," he said. "Nothing not expected."

Then we took off through the portal and were back in our world. I told Luke to meet us at Tara's place and then we would go home. So we landed back on Tara and Satar's world. We asked them if they could leave their portal open for our animals and insects to explore and maybe find a new place to live or find food since we didn't have that much for them on our planet.

"Sure," they said.

I told them that we had sensors along the portal walls and that we would close the portal from our end if something was coming.

"Thanks," they said.

Then Luke and I took off and headed back home. But first, we flew around looking for some of the birds we had let loose. Sure enough, our seagulls were foraging on the beach. They had found what looked like snails or maybe some small fish in the shallows.

"That is a good sign," I said to Luke. "Do you see any of the other birds we let loose?"

"No," Luke said.

"Well, then, let's go home," I said.

"I'm right behind you," Luke bellowed out.

"Sometimes, Luke, if you weren't my brother, I would smack you."

"That has never stopped you before," Luke said.

"What do you mean, Luke? I never hit you, except in football."

"I know, Orian. Just messing with you."

Soon we were at the shuttle bay where two small humanoids were standing. *How cute*, I thought to myself. We landed and then went down the elevator to our house below.

"Where have you guys been?" Doreen asked with a stern voice.

"What do you mean, Doreen?"

"You have been gone for days!"

"We have not," Luke said. "We have only been gone a few hours."

"Yes, really," I said to Doreen. "Maybe that world has different time than ours. We were only gone a few hours in Sanfe's world, but we have been gone days in our world."

"We will have to work on that," Mark said.

"I am going to take a nap," I said.

"Me too," said Luke. "See you gals in a couple of hours then."

Off we went while Amanda, Beth, and Shane worked on beehives to let a swarm of honey bees loose. I liked seeing the new life that we had put on the planet. The cattle and pigs were ready to be put out to pasture soon too. I would have Shane and a couple humanoids clear eighty acres to start with and then plant some alfalfa for the cows to eat and some corn and soybeans for the hogs. It seemed like the soil had some kind of growth hormone in it. Our corn and other vegetables that we planted in the garden grew faster than I had ever seen.

Shane started getting ready to cut down some of the mushroom trees, and Amanda said "Why don't we see if the mushroom trees are edible."

"Good idea. They do look kind of like the mushrooms that we had on Earth, only bigger and more beautiful."

I had one of the humanoids bring in a piece of one to have it analyzed, and we found out that they were edible. I told Shane to put some of the mushroom trees into our freezer for us to eat. Just one mushroom would last months. I told Shane to leave most of the mushrooms alone and plow and plant around them.

"Plow and plant mostly where the bamboo grasses are," I said.

"Okay," Shane said. "It will take quite a few hours to complete all the tasks that you have set for me to do."

"It's okay. Shane, just clear land, and for a change, let's have a normal day. Then plant seeds on the other half of our long days."

I went into the main viewer room and looked at some of the logs that we had put in and kind of went over all that we had done and where we had gone so far on the planet. We had been in a lot of fights, gotten swallowed by a fish, and had a huge war against the Vipeters, and then been in just a small fight on the last planet that we had ventured onto.

I thought of Loper and his race of Celanas people. I still thought something was a little fishy about his race, so I decided I would fly alone with a couple of humanoids have a sit-down talk with Loper and his people. I wanted to see his operations. I would have to gain more of his trust before I could really get to know all of his plans and complete operation.

So I got up and took Mark and a couple other humanoids to go to Loper's world. I wanted to find him and get to know more about his people and his operations. We already had our force field belts on, so we climbed into our ship, opened the shuttle bay doors, and off we went. This time the computer had made my starship a beautiful, shiny color. My spacecraft was also longer so it could hold more cargo and humanoids. It was a lot slimmer than the other starships that I had.

"Mark," I said, "when did they build this?"

"The humanoids and the computer have worked on it for about a week."

"Thank you, Computer," I said, and then off we went.

We went through the portal that went to Loper's world, and we stopped at the entertainment center to talk to Lepkwod the bartender. I wanted to see if he had found out anything more about Loper's operations. He said he had.

"They control all the power that this world consumes. If Loper wanted to, he could shut off all the power to any city or to the whole planet if he wanted to. But Loper has been good to us for a long time now."

Mark and I sat down, and I had a cherry drink. I asked Mark if he thought that Doc would allow someone to have complete power over an entire planet.

"I don't think so," Mark said. "Being that this is not our world, I would stop any wrongdoing to anyone, any planet, when something is controlling people's rights and dictating how they lived. Mark told me that it was almost impossible for us to be able to fight whole planets with just humanoids and Shane and Luke.

"Yes," I said, "but we will create more starships and more humanoids. I think I will call them humanoids from now on. I will have to name all the humanoids. The humanoids are just like real human beings.

"I'm sorry. I got off track there, Mark. But do you mind if we call them and you humanoids?"

"It would be an honor to be called human," Mark said. "And back to your idea, Orian, I think we should stay out of other worlds' problems."

"Well, if you think that way, Mark, why did we help the Leamarkes and the Anomies defeat the Vipeters?"

"That was a whole different situation," Mark said. "A complete planet was going to be destroyed by beasts that had no value for life."

"I guess you're right, Mark. But I still would like to see the Celanas people get to have some of the control over the power supply of the planet."

"I am just here to help you," Mark said, "But please takes my advice and stay out of other worlds' problems."

"But, Mark, it might be like fate that we have been to three different planets now and have united the three worlds together somewhat already."

"Yes, it is nice what you have done, Orian. I think that your idea of uniting the entire world together is a good one."

"Lepkwod, do you know or I can find, Loper?"

"Yes, he's probably at the main plant in his office this time of day."

"Where is his office?" I asked Lepkwod.

"About two hundred miles due south of here. So if you just head straight south, you will find him," Lepkwod said.

I asked what the building looked like, and he told me that I would see a lot of black smoke coming out of the huge plant.

"You can see it for many miles," he said.

"Okay, Mark. Let's leave this town and go find Loper. This may be a good chance to get to know his operations better."

So into the starship we got. We pointed the ship straight south and left the city to go find Loper's plant.

We took our time flying to Loper's plant so we could see more of this planet and see how the people live. Soon we saw a lot of smoke filling the air with gases of unknown type coming from a large factory size building.

"Mark, that must be Loper's place," I said.

"Yes, I believe it is," Mark said.

We took the starship down to the ground and landed at the power plant. Then we got out, and I told some of the humanoids to protect the ship at all costs.

"You will know if we are in trouble or not. I had over twenty humanoids in the ship, but just Mark and I went into the plant. It took several minutes before someone would open the door so we could enter. I kept telling them through the speakerphone that I was there to see Loper.

"Just tell him that Orian and some of his friends are here."

Finally, the door opened, and we entered. I said hello to the Celanas people.

"Where is Loper's office?" I asked.

The Celanas people pointed me in the right direction to Loper's office. We finally got to Loper's office and knocked on the door. We asked Loper if we could come in.

"Come on in," Loper said. "I will show you some of what I do here."

"That would be nice," I said to Loper. "I would like to see your operation and how the mining equipment is working for you."

"This is the main command center for the whole world's power supply. We have underground cables that travel around this whole world to our neighbors where the sun shines six months straight out of the year. We supply all of our cities here with power."

"Have you ever shut the power off to the cities around you or to any other part of the planet?" I asked.

"Oh no," Loper said. "That would be indecent of us."

I told Loper that I agreed, but I also told Loper that, before it got destroyed, the whole planet we lived on wouldn't allow one company to own all rights of the power supply. No other corporation would be able to command the whole world's commodities." I did tell Loper that some of the people were concerned about him having so much power over their electricity supply and how much they had to pay to keep their lights on.

"Well, we have to charge that much," Loper said in a kind of angry voice. "Why are you people asking so many questions about how our world works?"

"No reason," I said to Loper. "I was just wondering how your world operates and how you operate the corporations on the planet. Right now, we live a simple life and are interested in combining all of the worlds on our planet together at some point in time."

"I don't think that will ever happen," Loper said.

"Why do you say that, Loper? Have you ever met people from different worlds besides the one that we were fighting on together as one?"

"Yes," Loper said. "They were nice people, but the main thing was we were still mad at the Vipeters for destroying our planet. That is the only reason that I sent so many of my men to their death. But if they were in a fight with different people on their world, we would not have interfered, and we would have let the superior race win."

"Loper, does that mean that if some other people on this planet wanted to take control of this world and your power plant that we shouldn't help you if they were winning?"

"It would never happen," Loper said. "We are too powerful for the other people on this planet to fight us or to think that they would win."

"But you're saying, just in case, Loper, if the tables were turned and we were friends as we are now, that we should not interfere and help you conquer your enemy?"

"Yes," Loper said. "But we would welcome you to join our fight and be able to win a quick victory if war ever did break out on this planet."

"Loper, would you be willing to take a short trip with me to another world, a whole different world than the one that you live on now?"

"Yes," Loper said. "Can I take some I people with me?"

"That is fine," I said to Loper.

Loper gathered a few of his men. I told Loper to make sure that they were armed and ready to fight over nothing on the planet that I was taking them to, so Loper's men gathered their weapons and climbed into our starship. We took off and flew fast to the portal. We left to go back to our world and then made a quick right turn and headed for the portal for Sanfe's house.

We landed in the tall grass right next to Sanfe's hut. Mark, Loper, and I got out of the ship and went to Sanfe's hut. Sanfe's wife, who was named Teresa, answered the door.

"Oh, Orian, Mark, nice to see you again You and your friends, come on in. What are you doing on our planet today?"

I told her we wanted Sanfe to go with us to the city Plaxer, where we had encountered all the other ships and where we had had some fights and arguments.

"Oh, Orian, Sanfe is in the city now trying to buy some parts for his speeder. He is also trying to sell some parts that he salvaged from destroyed ships on this planet."

"Okay," I said to Teresa. "We will leave and see if we can catch up with Sanfe."

We all said our good-byes to Teresa and her family. We got back in the starship and headed toward the city Plaxer. As we traveled to the city, I told Loper and his men to be very careful in the city as they would meet different aliens from all over the universe.

"Wow. All over the universe?" Loper said.

"Yes," I said. "This is an entertainment and refueling world. So you will meet all different kinds of people and different looking. Nothing like you have seen on your planet."

"You have been here, Orian?"

"Yes, Loper, and we had some fights in the city with different aliens trying to dismantle our ships. But with our force fields and humanoids using our guns on stun, we stopped the thieves from trying to steal our ships."

Soon we landed in Plaxer, and we parked almost on the same landing pad we had parked on before. We were greeted by Tapor, who was the same person who had greeted us before.

"Well, hello again," he said. "Been a long time, beauty. Fuel?"

"No," I said. "I'm here to see Sanfe. Tapor, do you know where Sanfe is?"

"Yes, I do. You see that large building off to your left?"

"Ah, yes. I see it," I said. "Okay, we will get out and go over and see if we can't find Sanfe."

I told four of the humanoids to guard the ship like they had before while we had gone into the city.

"Well, everybody, let's get out of the ship. I will show you the city. But be careful. Try not to even bump into any alien that might want start a fight."

"Why do you come here if this place is so dangerous?" Loper asked.

"Because," I said, "along with the bad, there are so many nice people that come here. Those are the people that we communicate with and have an occasional dinner and a few drinks with," I told Loper. "They have alcohol in these bars, but we don't drink, so we have sweet drinks that taste pretty good. But I don't know what they're made of." I laughed.

"I will have some of the strong drinks here," Loper said.

"Here, have some zarra," I said to Loper. "This is money that you can use on this planet." Then I remembered that I had two small humanoids on the ship that belonged to Sanfe; I know how happy he'd be when he got them.

As we walked on the busy streets trying to find Sanfe, different aliens commented on how we looked at them and were almost going to start a fight. I noticed that they were some of the same people who had tried to steal from our ship. We had defeated them easily.

I looked at them and said, "Good morning. Nice day, right?"

"Oh yes," they said. "Nice day."

"Oh, and guys," I said, "leave our ship alone today or we will use deadly force."

Then Loper bumped into an alien as we were walking down the street. The alien turned around and hit Loper with a right hook to the face. Down went Loper. Loper's men then attacked the alien and gave him a good licking. Then other aliens joined in the fight. We were drawn into the fight as well. I was getting hit, but my force field belt stopped all blows. We had our force fields hit the aliens first, and we were knocking them down left and right. There were about forty aliens in the fight, and they were fighting amongst themselves as we are fighting with the aliens that were attacking us. A lot of the aliens left me and the humanoids alone, because we were untouched by their punches. Loper and his men were getting hit, but they were doing a pretty good job of fighting back.

Soon everyone was exhausted. The fighting stopped, and everyone, including us, went into the bar to get some refreshments. As long as Loper and his friends stayed with us at our table, we were fine. The aliens didn't want to fight with us. We had kind of become the bosses of this town because of our technology. I told Loper that, on Earth, the technology was terrible compared to what we had now and that our ship's computer kept us updated and created more technology as the time passed over all those years that we were frozen in space.

"I wish I knew what two hundred fifty billion years meant in our time," Loper said.

When one of Loper's men went up to the bar to buy another drink, one of the aliens pointed a weapon at him and said, "No ugly people are going to stand next to me." Loper's man ordered his drink anyway and told the guy next to him that he was too ugly to be calling him ugly. Then they got into a gun battle. By the time Loper's man got killed in the fight, the other alien, which looked like an alligator, had been mortally wounded as well.

"Let's grab our man and take him to the ship," Loper said." I will wait for you at the ship while you go and find your friend Sanfe."

"Okay," I said. "I told you this place was rough, and I told your people to just ignore what these aliens say to you. Just tell one of the humanoids to open the ship and allow you in. I will go get Sanfe so I can give him his humanoids and receive payment so we have more money to spend on this planet."

Mark and I headed off toward a large building to find Sanfe. Once we got to the large building, we went in. It was like a flea market or auction. Everything was available for sale. I walked up and down the aisles looking for Sanfe. Finally, I saw him bargaining at one of the auctions.

"Hello, Sanfe."

"Well, Orian and Mark, hello. It has been a while since we've seen you."

"In our world, it's only been two days."

"That is all?"

"Yes," I said. "For some reason when we go to your planet and then back to ours, the time difference is extreme. By the way, Sanfe, I have your humanoids."

"I thank you," Sanfe said. "Will you help me carry some of the parts that I bought back to the landing pad?"

"Sure, Sanfe. And I will ask the humanoids to help as well. Mark and the other humanoids can carry the heavy stuff while you and I can take a walk back to the landing pads. I will introduce you to Loper."

I told him about Loper and his people and that one of them had gotten into a fight at a tavern and had been shot and killed. "The other alien, I think, is dead by now also."

"Well, it happens all time here," Sanfe said. "We sand dwarfs are always safe on this planet, since we supply most of the fuel and the food the aliens put in their cargo bays before they leave."

We finally got to the ship, and I asked Sanfe how he was going get all his supplies back to his house.

"On a speeder. You know, Orian, I didn't bring my ship to the city, because I didn't plan on buying so much. I almost have enough now to complete my own ship."

"Sanfe, put your stuff in our cargo bay, and we will take it back for you. And any time that you need to carry large amounts of parts back to your home, we will help you. Just come and get us, and we will help you.

"Sanfe," I continued, "these are Loper and his friends. Loper, this is Sanfe."

"Hello. Nice to meet you, Sanfe," Loper said.

"Loper, it is nice to meet you too." Sanfe went on to say how sorry he was about Loper's loss. We talked for a while, but we had to leave to get Loper's friend back to his wife so she could grieve.

"But first," I told Sanfe, "I will drop the humanoids and your parts at your house, and we will come back soon."

Sanfe took off toward home on his speeder, and we got into the ship and followed Sanfe. We got to Sanfe's home and unloaded his parts next to the ship that he was building. I also unloaded the humanoids.

They went up to Sanfe and said, "Hello, Sanfe, we will do anything that you program us to do."

Sanfe was impressed and paid us many zarra for the humanoids. Then we said our good-byes and took off to go back to Loper's land on planet Saphra.

We pointed the starship toward the portal. There was a sign, like for all the other portals we had visited so far that translated to say, "This way to the source." That was it; there was no opening that I could see, just a sign that seemed embedded in the air.

Through the portal, we flew, waving at the girls. We flew through Loper's portal and took him and his men back to his factory. We unloaded the dead Celana and said good-bye to Loper.

Before I left, I asked Loper, "What aliens should I have decided to help in that fight? The planet Zipam or the city of Minatar."

"Well, us," Loper said.

"You don't believe in saving a world that has problems like planet Zipam has?" I asked.

We said good-bye to Loper, and off we went to see where the mining operation was and how the equipment we had given to Loper was working. Loper had told us where the mining operation was and how to get there, so we flew to the west until we found a huge hole in the ground, just like the mining operations back on Earth.

Then we saw our mining equipment working hard, picking up the materials, and then flying back to the plant.

"Kind of a cool operation," I said to Mark.

"But burning the fuel here on this planet will destroy the air many years from now if they don't find an alternative energy source," Mark said.

When we got back to our house, the girls asked us again why we were gone for so many days.

"According to our new watch," I said, "we were only gone for half a day. Time changes when we go to one planet and then back home." Then I told them about what had happened to one of Loper's friends in the bar. "Someday in the future," I told them, "I am going to create humanoids to keep the peace on that planet and in that town."

"Not a good idea," Mark said.

"Why is that?" I asked.

"Because you shouldn't interfere with the way each world works."

"Yes," Doreen said. "It is good to have friends in each world, but please be careful, Orian. Don't go too far to change their ways of life."

"Doreen, let's go to the source and talk and just relax for a while."

"That sounds nice, Orian. Let's go," Doreen said, then she asked if I wanted to take a lunch.

"Yes, I am kind of hungry," I said. "Then we can have a nice meal at the source and try to figure out what makes that power source so important to all the worlds that I have visited so far."

"Yes, I would like to know that too, Orian," said Doreen.

While Doreen went to cook our lunch, I went to the shuttle bay and grabbed a small craft that would fit Doreen, me, Mark, and a few humanoids, just in case we got in trouble. Then I flew the small craft down to the house and landed. I went into the kitchen and saw Doreen cooking some mushroom stems and some meat and packing bread so she could make us sandwiches.

"Doreen?" I asked "How is Shane coming on the fields?"

"You were gone so long, it's all been plowed and cleared," Doreen said. "And most of the seeds are planted, and some like the grass seeds are already coming up. I think, within a week that we can let the cattle and the pigs out into the pasture. The humanoids have the fence up so the cattle can't get out."

"Where is Shane now?"

"He and Amanda and Beth are taking a nap, and Luke went to see Tara and Satar."

"Luke went all alone?" I asked.

"No, Orian, he took a couple of humanoids with him, and he is fine. So don't worry about him. If it was Shane, you wouldn't be worried."

"Yes, I know Doreen. Shane is the biggest of all us boys, and he doesn't seem to have the interest that Luke and I share."

"I think he would rather be with Amanda and helping Beth with the animals and starting wildlife on this new world."

"I agree, Doreen. At least we are all different in certain ways. I never thought that I would have the guts to stand up to different aliens and get into fights. I was never that way on Earth. I think Doc reprogrammed me during our flight to be stronger than I was on Earth. Boy, Doreen, does that smell good," I said. "I almost feel like eating now. But I think it will be more fun to eat at the source."

"That is our plan," Doreen said. "And I am about ready to fill the picnic basket, so we can go, okay?"

"Doreen, I will meet you at the ship. It is in the backyard. I will check all systems so we can go."

Doreen finally met me at the ship, and we both got in. Mark and the other humanoids were already in the ship. After we climbed on board, we headed the ship toward the source. Once we were at our destination, we landed the ship, and Doreen got out the picnic basket. After we got off the ship, we walked toward the source.

I still couldn't believe the beauty of the crystal that circled the force or the big hole that all the water flowed to from all the rivers around our world. It was truly a marvelous place. Doreen, Mark, and I walked over to the source, and there we saw nice place to set up a picnic area. Doreen and I sat down. We got the food out of the picnic basket and ate the wonderful food that Doreen had cooked.

"This is delicious, Doreen. I think some of this meat is better than what we had on Earth."

"Yes." she says. "I think it has more protein and vitamins. Orian, your eyes are turning blue now too."

"They are?" I asked. "And your eyes are dark blue, Doreen. But it makes you look more beautiful."

"Thank you, Orian. I needed to hear that. You have been gone so long and so many times. I really missed you."

I told Doreen that I did like the way the time changed when we went to different planets and returned. "But really, Doreen, it only happens when we go to planet Zipam."

While we were eating, I asked Doreen, "Do you feel anything strange?"

"Yes, I do," Doreen said. "I feel a sense of safety, and I feel more emotional. How about you, Orian?"

"Yes, I feel the same. It must be something to do with the source."

"I know."

"It makes you feel close to all worlds, doesn't it, Doreen?"

I still wondered why the different aliens came to the source. I saw one alien from Loper's world dump wood-like ashes into the hole, and I also saw Satar put something into the hole of the source.

"I think that this source has something to do with the dead of the aliens of all of different worlds. But, Doreen, that is just my idea. I do feel closer to something more powerful than me."

"Yes, I feel the same way," Doreen said me.

After Doreen and I ate our nice lunch, we got back into the small craft and headed back home. I wanted to discuss some of my ideas with the rest of the family, so when I got home, I radioed Shane and Luke. I told them to meet us back home in a couple of hours. I asked Luke to bring Satar and Tara back when he came.

I was worried about the Celanas having so much power over their entire planet. I felt sorry for the people and aliens that had to pay so much for power. I wanted to get Tara and Satar's opinions before I did anything drastic. I was thinking of having our computer make a power plant out of our Taperian force erupter drive. Just a small unit would power an entire city. I would do it for free or maybe just for a little bit of money, so we would have something to spend at the shops there.

Soon Luke came with Tara and Satar, and Shane finished up in the fields when it started to rain all of a sudden. It rained hard this time. Our force fields were up-to-date for the lightning strikes if they were at the same intensity as before. We all sat out on a lanai, watching the rain come down and the lightning strike all over. It was shaking our house and our ship as lightning hit the force fields.

"How's the force field holding, Mark?"

"Fine, Orian, the shields are still at one hundred percent."

Then down came several more lightning strikes in a row, and the whole house just shook from all the energy that the lightning bolts were delivering to our force fields.

"I have never seen it rain this hard, and I have never been in your world when the weather was this bad."

"With those last strikes, the shields went down to eighty percent," Mark said. "But they have rebounded to ninety-five percent and are holding."

The thunder was loud, and the ground shook beneath our feet. At times, we had to hold on to our seats so we wouldn't fall off them when the ground shook. Doreen and Amanda got all of us something to drink, and I talked to Satar and Tara about my idea of starting a power plant on planet Saphra. Both Tara and Satar said I shouldn't interfere. I told them how some of the people were suffering and that I didn't believe any one person should have complete power of the world's power supply.

"This would never have happened on my old planet, but Mark and the computer tell me to stay out of it, but I think that I'll have the computer make a Taperian force erupter power generator that would last a lifetime of the planet's existence. I would only do this for one city to see how that project works."

"I don't know," said Satar. "You might interrupt the balance of power that the planet now has."

"You might be right, Satar, but I still think the people should have a choice on where they get their power from. So I think I'm going to do it. I know I'll make Loper angry, but I hope not angry enough to fight. That is the last thing that I want to happen. Loper is my friend. Computer?"

"Yes, Orian?"

"Make a small Taperian force erupter power plant so I can take it to the planet Saphra."

"If that is what you want," said the computer.

"I think you're making a mistake," Mark said.

"Before I install the new drive after it is ready, I think I am going to talk to Loper. See if he wants to share in the distribution of power. Also, we would be helping the planet's air quality."

"I just hope you know what you're doing, Orian."

"I will be extra careful how I talk to Loper. We don't want war with the Celanas or for innocent people to get hurt or killed over my actions."

After the drive was finished, I would go to meet with the people in the city of Minatar. I would just see what the people thought of having two power plants available to power their city and beyond, with some of their control added to Loper's. The power should not being completely owned by one race of people but should be owned by the city of Minatar.

Chapter Eleven

"Satar and Tara, you want to come with me tomorrow night to talk to some of the people in the city of Minatar? You can see what I am talking about."

"Yes, we will go, but only as observers. We are not going to give you any advice until after we leave planet Saphra."

"That's the deal?" I said. "Meet me here at your morning time and please ring the bell at our force field. That will wake us up and let us know that you are here."

The rain was letting up then; I didn't see any more lightning. It will make our seeds that we had planted grow.

"Luke, will you fly Tara and Satar back home?"

"Sure. Let's go, guys," he said, and off they went.

"Well, Shane, what do you think of my idea?"

"I don't know, Orian. I think you're taking a big chance. But if you think it's right, then we will try to do it your way."

"Computer, how long will it take to build a Taperian force erupter?"

"That will take some time. I think I can have it finished in thirty-six hours."

"That would be great," I said. "I will take it with me when I go to Minatar. Later, I will show it to Loper after bringing Satar and Tara back to their world. Then I will go back and try to make a deal with Loper."

Then I went to my quarters and asked Doreen to join me so I could discuss the idea further with her. I asked her if she wanted to come with me to Minatar to talk to the people there to see how they felt.

"Doreen, if I do get in trouble, the only thing that bothers me is that the people in Minatar do not have any weapons. And if Loper wants to fight, it would be just me and the humanoids against his whole army. I will not involve Luke or Shane in this fight if it happens," I said. "Now that the rain has stopped, let's send our mining equipment to get more material to fill up the construction bay. This way we will have enough material to make more humanoids, starships, and other necessities if needed."

"Orian, it sounds like you want to fight," Doreen said.

"No, I don't, Doreen. I just want people to have freedom like we had on Earth in America. Loper has made that planet into a socialistic state. And I am against that. I know our numbers are low as yet, but in order for us to survive; we have to make peace and be friends with every alien that we meet, even if it means a small fight between their race and ours. You are looking at me like I have changed, Doreen."

"You have," she said. "You're not a teenager anymore. Even though you're only seventeen, it seems like you are now a lot older."

"I'm sorry. I don't want to be a kid again. Things have changed. We no longer have parents, and we have children on the ship that are younger than you and I. So we have to be older and stronger for them. I promise you, Doreen, that I will try to be a teenager again, so we can go out on dates and just have fun. You see, Doreen, my theory is if we help these people save money and have a choice, we will have more fun in their towns and be freer to shop and maybe even live on their planet someday if we have to.

"But for now, Doreen, if I have to be older and make choices, then I will have to do so. But I don't want our relationship to diminish. Somehow, someday, Doreen, I want you to be my wife. We can go through a ritual in Satar's world or maybe use the computer as a preacher from its memory banks."

"Are you proposing to me, Orian?"

"Yes, I guess I am," I said. "Let's make it a year from now when we turn eighteen."

"Then I accept your proposal, Orian. I would be happy to be your wife someday. But please don't get yourself killed trying to unite all these planets and worlds."

"Well, Doreen," I said, "I think I am going to take a nap. I may help Shane out in the field tomorrow. I could put up some stakes in the new corrals for the cattle and hogs. I might like to do some farming myself. Care to help me tomorrow?"

"Sounds fun, Orian. The way things grow here on this world, we will need more room. Even the oak trees and the cranberry trees and the apple trees are growing at a tremendous rate. It takes seven years for trees on earth to produce fruit, but I think these trees will be able to produce fruit in less than a year of our time."

"You're kidding."

"No, I'm not," she said.

"You have been so busy and haven't seen all that we have done while you were off on all those different worlds."

"All right, Doreen. Tomorrow, I will look at everything you have done while I'm waiting for my new power plant to be built. And we will set up more fencing for the cattle."

"We will have to build a barn," Doreen said, "so the animals can get out of the rain and have shelter during these large thunderstorms. Maybe a force field over the barn too so that the lighting won't hurt our livestock."

"Sounds good, Doreen, and I will see you in the morning—or at least in eight hours when I finally wake up. Before I go to bed, let me ask the computer something, Doreen. "Computer, on this planet, have you figured out how long a year is and how we age on this planet?"

"Yes, I have," the computer said. "All the probes sent back information on the orbit of our planet and the speed at which it rotates and travels around our suns. I figure every twenty-six Earth years, you age only a one year on this planet. I am in the process of making a new calendar for this world of ours and also a watch that will tell you what time of day it is. The way I see it," the computer said, "I think you would get used to working and staying up the full time the sunlight is out. You only need eight hours of sleep during our darkest periods."

I had a good night's rest, and then I got up. I noticed that Shane, Amanda, Beth, Luke, and Doreen were still sleeping, so I decided to check on the progress of the new power plant that I was creating. I remembered that the day was for Doreen and that we were going to make more pasture space. Besides, the computer said it would take about thirty-six hours to complete the new power generation system. The computer said it will only be the size of a small generator. I had the computer update me on the progress.

"It will probably be another twenty-four hours, Orian," the computer said. "Then I'll be finished."

I also asked the computer to send Mark and some of the humanoids to put fencing material in the cargo ship.

"We can take it out to build our fence today."

"By the time you and your family eat breakfast, shower, and get dressed," the computer said, "I will have the cargo ship loaded with all of material that you will need for the fencing that you plan on putting up."

Mark arrived, and he saw me sitting in the living room going through the logs. We took on Loper's planet and were still wondering if I was doing the right thing. Mark and I discussed my plan. I was getting ready to maybe wake up the rest of the family, but then I decided to let them sleep in, not knowing what time they had all gone to bed.

"I think Loper will go for the new generating plant so he doesn't have to use the mine much, not having to refuel the Taperian force erupter generator for life on this planet or beyond. If he or anybody else tried to copy my drive, it would self-destruct and probably kill hundreds of people in the explosion that would follow. If the Taperian drive gets fooled with, it would self-destruct. I think that's enough thinking for today. I will discuss it with Loper tomorrow when I go to his planet. I will talk to him and the rest of the Celanas people about my idea, but I will probably try to force the idea on to Loper," I said.

Then I felt movement; well, actually I heard the rest of the gang struggling to get out of bed.

"Wake up on this beautiful day," I said.

Finally the all of them came to the kitchen area, and I could see them from the living room.

"Good morning, folks," I said. I asked Doreen what she was going to cook for breakfast she told me bacon and eggs, so I made my way to the kitchen and asked her if we should take some food with us just in case we got hungry while we were putting up defenses for the animals.

I had noticed that, underneath the mushrooms on the ground, there was a mossy substance that was about knee high.

The computer had said, "I will check the quality of the underbrush," and then had told me that it was a hedge. It would be good food for the cattle to feed upon. I just hoped we wouldn't ruin our ecosystem.

Finally, we were all up. The two suns in the sky were still shining brightly into our house. It would be another five days before nightfall would come.

I asked Doreen if she was still interested in working with me that day, and she said that she would enjoy that very much. Doreen also said that working with me reminded her of the farming that we had done on Earth.

"After breakfast, Doreen, why don't you make us a lunch that we can take with us?"

Luke told me that if I got into a firefight he would stand at my side and fight.

"Thank you," I told him, "but this is my war if it ever happens. Luke and Shane, I need you here to take care of the girls while I am gone."

Then Doreen said, in an excited voice, that I had proposed marriage to her the night before. But I told the crew that wouldn't happen until we turned eighteen according to the planet's new calendar system that the computer had created for us while we were sleeping. As usual, I had gotten up early again, and I was looking forward to working together. Even though I'd known

Doreen all her life, I thought to myself that I was a lucky person to be able to marry such a good girl. *That will make me happy. In fact, I know I'll be happy for the rest of my life.*

I asked Mark if we could have a double ceremony and if any of the people of the other worlds got married on our planet.

"I really enjoy your company, Doreen," I said. "You and I can have a beautiful life on this planet. We should keep in an updated calendar system of all the birthdays. I have all of our good pictures and take care of the pictures that we have in storage on the ship."

Keep the Leamarke parking space to one of the three stalls. That's to make our spacecrafts safer against people stealing our starships or if one of us got mugged again. So next time we will meet with all information on your trip to America. Some of the humanoids were a little disappointed in my system, but I reassured them that I wouldn't do it much anymore. I even wished that one of the planets we entered would see me for who I am. I was not a butcher. Mostly, I was a leader. I had much compassion toward people, and their wonderful faces have been missed. And to watch them . . . he eyes the ball better than Luke plays.

I was just thinking of the meeting with Loper and his men. They might get too busy fighting for lower prices of their electric bills and sharing control over the power plant to make it easier for the aliens like Sanfe. While thinking of all these options, I finally got tired, climbed in my bed, and fell fast asleep. I normally wouldn't take a nap, but I had so many worries going through my head. I was kind of manic, so I didn't sleep much anyway. I got back up and walked to the house and asked Doreen if she was ready to go to work on the new fence for the cattle.

Doreen and I got to talking about where to put the fence, wondering if we needed to clear more land or just let the cattle graze off the underbrush or even if we could have the cattle graze in a large area of the lush ground underneath all ferns and the mushroom trees. Doreen and I decided to put a large fence up for the cattle and let them graze on all the undergrowth that was in the world, so we got into the spacecraft and took a couple of humanoids with us just in case we might run into some trouble putting the fence in. Doreen told me that she had packed us a big lunch.

We would start to put the fence where the barn was going to be built. Then we would build it about a half mile down and a mile across the back. We thought that should be enough for the cattle that we planned on having.

"Doreen," I said, "there were gloves in the spacecraft underneath the seat, if you need a pair."

Doreen went and got the gloves while the humanoids and I started to unload the fencing. The fencing that we were using gave out more electrical shocks than the electric fence that we had had on Earth. It was made of laser beams instead of wire to keep the cattle and hogs in.

Doreen and I worked for about eight hours, and we got the fencing done. Then we activated the fence to see if it worked, and sure enough, it worked just fine. As we climbed back into the starship, we left the doors open, because it was such a beautiful day. We had our force fields and everything off.

Then all of a sudden, Doreen flew forward, and I saw what looked like the arrows the Indians used to have. It had hit her, and I noticed she was in a lot of pain. I knew I had to get her to the infirmary quickly to have the arrow taken out. It looked as if Doreen had lost a lot of blood.

Thinking quickly, I broke the back of the arrow off and pulled the rest of the arrow out of her chest. I turned the force fields on and turned around.

With the ship pointing toward where the arrow had come from, I saw hundreds of aliens all with the same type of weapon, and they fired their arrows at a tremendous speed. Arrows were bouncing off the ship's force field. Quickly, I fired some stun guns at them. As I did this, they were just knocked down to the ground, but they got right up again.

I sped toward the starship as fast as I could go to get Doreen to the doctor in the spaceship; they had to operate on her and do anything so we wouldn't lose her. It didn't take me long to get Doreen to the hospital, because Shane and Luke were in the living room when I yelled for help. Doreen spent at least six hours in surgery. The doctors were giving her blood transfusions because she had lost so much, and the blood she was getting was from me, because I have O-positive blood and can donate blood to anyone. I noticed that we were short on real blood, so I decided that, every other day, I would give a pint of blood and save it in the sick bay. I would have to check on Shane and Luke's blood type to see if they were O-positive too. Then we could all replenish the blood supply.

After a while, Doreen came to. She said she wasn't in much pain, and the doctor had done a painless operation.

"You just rest, Doreen," I said. "I am going to go out and confront those cockroach-like creatures. They walk on two legs, have six arms, and can fire three arrows at the same time. They must have some defense on them to be able to shake the stun off so quickly."

I heard Amanda and Beth screaming, so told Doreen to stay and get well while I took care of those menacing people.

As I took the elevator down and went to our house, I looked at the outside force field. The creatures were firing arrows at the force field and trying to shoot over the top of it, but that was covered as well.

Luke got upset and said, "Orian, let's get going and destroy these creatures."

"First, Luke, put on the earpieces. We will talk to these people to find out why they attacked us."

We went to one of the smaller starships, and Luke and I got in. We were in the air in no time. What we did was keep firing the stun guns at them and fly just over their heads. This scared the creatures, and they backed away from the house. We landed outside the force field and turned our force field belts on high. Then we got out of the spaceship, and with our earpieces on, we could understand what they were saying. They were yelling for us to get off the world or they would destroy us.

I laughed at them and said, "You wouldn't have a chance in hell fighting us. We could wipe out your whole race in a matter of a few hours. We want peace here, now and forever."

All of a sudden, the leader spoke up and asked me to call him Himbe of the Thine people.

"Himbe, are you the leader?" I asked him in a stern voice. "Why did you shoot at women? Why not me? Or at our house?"

Himbe said that he was sorry. I told him that we had lost our world many years before and that we had finally found a planet that could support our lifestyle. We were asleep until our starship found a planet that could support life. I told Himbe that I had made peace with three worlds.

"Now they are not afraid to leave their portals open," I said. "They are cautious until we can meet every person that lives in these worlds and beyond the plasma field. Himbe, do you mind if we start over? Someday, may we have a key to your force field so we can enter and leave it at any time?"

Himbe told me that he was close to the portal on his left-hand side. I asked Himbe if he and some of his men wanted to come inside and have some refreshments.

"We can talk more," I said, "but you will have to put your weapons down before you can enter into our humble home."

Himbe selected five men to enter with him, and then I opened a gate and let the five in. I asked Luke if he would bring the starship back.

"No problem," Luke said.

"Himbe, you come into the starship with me. I would like to see you apologize to Doreen."

He agreed with his head bowed down. When we were in the starship, we took the elevator up to the medical area. Then we walked in to see Doreen and how she was doing.

Doreen opened her eyes and screamed.

"Why did you bring him in here?" she yelled.

"They had a misunderstanding," I said. "They saw our ship not too far from the source, so they were trying to scare us away. I showed them our power to put down their weapons, and now they're talking."

"I am very sorry that you got hurt," Himbe said to Doreen.

Doreen just stared at the strange creature. She was surprised that I had made friends with the creature that had been trying to hurt us. I could hear it in her voice.

"I think only you can do this, Orian: unite people."

"Yes," I said. "Doreen, from now on we have to keep our force field belts on and always activated when we are outside in the open."

"Force field belts?" Himbe asked.

"Yes," I said. "All our humanoids and humans have them. Our computer adjusts the power each time we are hit with a weapon. The computer compensates for it and upgrades weapons immediately, even the force field, if that should fail," I said. "Himbe, do you know what the source is for and how we're supposed to use it?"

"If you have faith, you will figure out as well," Himbe said.

"But how is it the lifeblood of all the worlds?"

"Because of the vast oceans. We have underground streams of water that seem to travel to our planet's water supply."

"Would that drain the oceans over the years?"

"No," said Himbe. "When it rains on our planet, the ground doesn't soak it up. It flows backward into your ocean."

"I have some work to do on planet Saphra through a different portal than yours, and there are a lot of nice people in all three worlds that I have explored so far."

I showed Himbe the war that we had fought, and he was amazed by the creatures we called Vipeters. After Himbe and I talked, he and his men left to go to the source and give their offering. The source was really starting to confuse me. I just wished somebody would give me a straight answer and explain to me the purpose of the source. How would we find out what the source really was?

Luke told me that Satar and Tara were leaving their portal open to let air into their world, so the trees and seeds we had planted would grow.

"Come to think of it," I said to Luke, "I never asked them if it rained on their planet! They must get rain on their planet; otherwise, they wouldn't have any vegetation."

I went back to sick bay to sit with Doreen for a while. When I got there, we held hands, and I told her how much I loved her.

"I'm sorry that I did not take more precautions and have our force field belts on."

Doreen said that it wasn't my entire fault; she always felt safe walking around our world.

"Maybe Himbe is right in thinking that we were here to destroy the force. No one has ever lived here before, as the legends go," Doreen said.

"Doreen, I hope you get better soon."

"I think I'll be up and running around tomorrow," Doreen said.

"How can that be?" I asked.

"The computer can create new tissue and bone if we break anything or get wounded. Our wounds will be corrected right away."

"Orian," the computer said, "I have a new addition to the ship that you might be interested in."

"What is that?" I asked the computer.

"We now have teleportation capabilities on the ship," the computer said. "If you get in trouble, I can teleport you back to the ship in a matter of a few seconds."

"Thanks, Computer.

"That is one task that your dad wanted me to work on until I got it right."

"You don't how good that makes me feel, Computer."

I told Doreen that I would wait another day before I went to Loper's world to show my new power supply to them.

"I would like you to come with me, Doreen, and you can see how I deal with aliens now."

"Orian," Doreen said, "you're getting such a big head. I think that your head will fall off your shoulders at some point in life."

"Doreen, when I sat in the mind chair and Doc gave me all of this knowledge, I just wonder if Doc programmed me to become older than my natural age of seventeen."

"Is that possible?" Doreen asked. "Because you sure know your way around these different worlds and seem to make friends everywhere you go."

"Thank you, Doreen. That was also nice of you," I said. "Sometimes, I worry that I'm not being a teenager and thinking of you as more than just a friend now. I want to make sure that I am there for you at all times. I feel like I've found my purpose in life, and that is to make sure that the human race survives and also to create peace between all the worlds."

Mark came into the room where I was sitting with Doreen. He told me that the Taperian force erupter plant was ready and was already being put in a starship.

"Thank you, Mark," I said. "I think I will go get Satar and Tara now and talk to the people in the city of Plaxer."

"Please be careful," Doreen said. "I don't know what I'd do without you. I think what you're doing is right for the people. And Orian, I am so proud of you, and I'm behind you a hundred percent."

"Mark, grab twenty-six fully armed humanoids to go with us to Loper's planet," I said. "I know that we have teleportation technology now; we will leave the portal doors open so that the main computer can interact with us and keep our defenses up-to-date."

Mark and I got into the nice, shiny starship with warp drives that was now capable of going at least thirty times the speed of light. Then we took off from the shuttle bay and headed toward Satar and Tara's world.

When we arrived, it was just early morning, so Satar asked us if we wanted some of their morning drink.

"Sure, Satar," I said. "Take your time, because Loper's world is kind of a dark world anyway."

As Satar and I were having coffee, Tara saw us and joined us. As we talked, Satar and Tara really enforced that they were not going to get involved in the project.

"Orian, we will go with you just for support."

"I thank you both," I said. "You can bring some of your people if you want."

"I think we will," said Satar.

"Oh Tara, by the way, how often do you get rain here?"

"Almost every day," Tara said.

"I don't understand," I said. "Most your planet is desert, and that usually means such dry air."

"I don't know," Tara said. "We must be getting moisture from someplace to make rain almost every day. I think the source is providing us with the rain."

I told Tara and Satar that I would figure out how the source worked sooner or later. "The rate that I am going," I said, "it will take me forever."

"I don't think so," said Satar. "One day, it will just come to you."

We finish our morning coffee and some treats for breakfast. Both Satar and Tara went out and gathered five men each to take to Loper's world. Then we all climbed into the starship. The first thing he noticed was how different the ship was compared to other shuttles that we owned.

I asked Mark to contact the computer and have the humanoids take the mining equipment out to get more out of the mountain and fill up the construction bay in the ship.

"Also, leave loads of ore and mining vehicles that we have and park them behind the house."

"Already done," Mark said.

"Thank you, Mark," I replied.

We soon got to Loper's portal. The first place to stop was in the city of Minatar. I would talk to the bartender Lepkwod and tell him about my idea. We parked the starship on top of one of the big buildings that looked like parking garages. When we all got out, I only took Mark with me. Satar and Tara took their ten men too. We finally arrived at the tavern called the Oak Mill Tavern. Lepkwod got us a table right away.

"Welcome, friends," he said. "What can I get you today?"

I told Lepkwod that I would just have a sweet drink and that I would pay for everyone's drinks. When Lepkwod brought us our drinks, I asked him how much he paid for power, and he told me that it took almost all his wages just to buy power.

"You have a conference room, Lepkwod?"

"Yes, I do," said Lepkwod.

"Can you have more people come to your conference room? I would like to talk to them. I have an idea that might solve some of your problems. I have in my possession a device that will power this whole city and pretty much the whole world for free. Of course, I would like to be able to get donations so that I can come to your city, and we can buy things from your markets."

"Boy, I don't know, Orian. We don't want to get into a fight with the Celanas. I told the people in the bar to go gather more people and friends and to pack the conference room as soon as we could." The bar was empty except for Lepkwod and my friends.

I told Lepkwod that I didn't want to fight with Loper either, but I told Lepkwod that, on our old planet Earth, it was against the law for one person or one company to own all of the power in our world. I told him that there were several different power companies that sold power to customers at a low cost because of competition.

"Your planet must have been beautiful."

"Yes, it was," I told Lepkwod. "In fact, here's a picture of Earth from a distance in space . . . one of the most beautiful planets. Lots of landmasses. But we destroyed our environment by burning fuels that came out of the ground. When you get around Loper's power plant you can hardly breathe. The air quality is so bad. And with my technology for free power, it will be managed by an important person in your city, not Loper. We have to stop a war from starting. I believe in what we call democracy. We have to help other people who don't have as much as other people do to survive better."

"That would be nice to have the new power supply," Lepkwod said. "When the sun is on our side for six months, it gets very warm here, and we have to cool our homes and businesses."

"I understand how you feel, Lepkwod."

Soon people started to head toward the conference room and take their seats. It only took a few minutes to fill up the whole place. There was standing room only. Lepkwod and I headed outside with a megaphone so that whole community could hear what I had to say.

"Just wait a minute," Lepkwod said. "I will connect the speaker system up."

"Okay, Lepkwod," I said.

"Hello, ladies and gentlemen. My name is Orian. I come from the world where the source is. We have advanced technology, and I heard how much you are paying for power from Loper. I want to have you people vote whether you want a new power supply that would be almost be free for you or not."

"Yes," they all yelled.

"Thank you. The generator I have will power your city above and beyond. It will take only one man to check the control panel every once in a while. I will give you some cases to store the extra power the Taperian force erupter generator creates, because it makes more power than it takes to run the machine. I will even come here and maintain the power source for you, if you would like me to."

"What about Loper?" a concerned citizen asked.

"I am going to talk to Loper after I leave here. I will try to come to an agreement with the Celanas. If Loper retaliates against you, I will be here at your side, fighting for your freedom and the right to own your own power company."

"Freedom," everybody yelled.

"If you all come with me to the roof my starship that is parked on, I will show you the generator."

"Yes," they said. "Let's go up and see what you have built for us."

Mark came with me, and the people followed us up to the parking garage. At first, the people were just amazed by my starship. I opened the cargo bay and showed them the small object I had made. I told the people that the generator is pollution-free and will produce more power than Loper's large plant.

I could tell that some of the people were worried about what Loper's reaction might be.

"Loper might retaliate in some way," I told them. "But Loper is my friend. I will work out some kind of deal. Even if he charges you a little bit for power, you will be a lot better off. I am going to go and try to convince Loper to allow power in this city and the countryside around you. You will have free power. Loper has the entire world at his fingertips right now, so he may not be happy with my decision to interfere with your justice system, making you more independent. Let's go back to the Oak Mill Tavern. I will gather my friends, and we will go talk to Loper.

"By the way, Lepkwod, where is your main power grid for the city?"

"It is just north of town on the left-hand side. You can't miss it. It has huge wires all around the site."

"Thank you, Lepkwod," I said. Then I asked my friends to come with me while I went to talk to Loper.

"We will stay here until you get back, okay?" Satar said.

"Okay," I said. I went off to the parking garage. I had Mark with me and twenty heavily armed humanoids, just in case. I decided to set up my Taperian force erupter generator at the substation and cut the power from Loper to try out my system.

"I don't know if that is a good idea," Mark said.

I told Mark that I was going to do it anyway.

Soon, I found the power grid substation and parked my starship. I had the humanoids carry my generator to the substation. Then I proceeded to tap into the grid to bypass Loper's power supply until I could get mine on line and working.

It took me just a little bit over an hour to get my system up and running. I disconnected Loper's power supply, and I put force fields around the substation so that no one could enter it and switch things around. My Taperian force erupter generator worked great. It wasn't even working hard to keep up with the power demand of the city and outlying areas.

Then I got into my starship and flew to Loper's plant. I had to find him or tell the Celanas what I had done for the city of Minatar. I arrived at the plant and knocked on the door. Loper came to the door with an angry face; he already knew what I had done in the city of Minatar.

"Everyone will still have to pay for their power," Loper said.

I got angry.

"Like hell you will, I have done you a big favor, and I was going to tell the people that it was your idea, so you would be treated like a king when you went to the city. One person can't own the whole world's power supply," I said. "I would make more generators for a price, so you don't have to mine ore and pollute the atmosphere and ruined your planet."

"You are just a kid. What do you know about how to run a country?"

"I believe in a free country and a world where everyone is equal."

Loper's men returned from the substation. They said that they had tried to get into the substation, but there was a strong force field blocking their way. Loper got really mad. He grabbed his weapon and pointed it at me.

"Go ahead and shoot," I said. "You won't hurt me. But I will kill you if you fire upon any of us."

Then the rest of the Celanas in the plant grabbed weapons. They all were pointing their guns at Mark and me. Mark summoned the rest of the humanoids to come to our aid. Soon, coming through the door were twenty more of us with guns drawn. All were pointing at Loper.

"Loper," I said, "I thought we were friends. I don't want to have to fight you. I just want some of this planet to have freedom and not have to pay so much for electricity."

Then one of the Celanas opened fire on us. Our force fields held, but there was still a shock to my system. All the humanoids opened fired upon the rest of the Celanas. Even though they had upgraded their defenses, our guns still penetrated their armor and force fields. They were slowly dying. I grabbed Loper and held him to the ground so he wouldn't get shot while the humanoids and the Celanas fought it out.

Some of the humanoid shields failed, and they were damaged beyond repair. We were doing a lot of killing of Loper's men as well.

"Mark," I yelled, "can you adjust our force fields to help protect the rest of our humanoids and you? Mark, please get out of the fight and come and sit here with Loper."

Mark did what he was told, and he adjusted the force fields to a different mode to protect us from the weapons of the Celanas people. We finally got the upper hand and drove the Celanas people out of the building. Their dead lay on the floor.

"Loper, was it worth it? We are at war now."

"I don't know," said Loper, "but thank you for saving my life."

I told him that I was sorry for the men he had lost in the battle, and he said the same for me, not knowing that the humanoids were not the same as me, not aware that they were robots. Then I told Loper not to go into the city to collect any more money and to stop treating people badly.

"I will be back and fight on their sides next time," I said. "Loper, if you come to your senses, come to our home for dinner, and we can figure out how I can help you with the power problem and my interference. I like you, Loper, but I tried to show you how a world was without law and how dangerous it was. If you get the people to trust you, you will be able to make plenty of money. But before I am finished, I will divide your power plants up and put in more of my free fuel generators."

"If you do that, we will stay at war," Loper replied.

"But, Loper," I said, "that is a war that you won't win, and a lot of your people will die. Just let me show you how a democratic government can work for you. The whole world and you can choose to be elected to be a king of your world. You can do what the majority of the people want. Well, I am leaving now, Loper. I hope that you will change your mind."

I had Mark load the dead humanoids into the starship, and then off we went back to the city to pick up our friends and tell the people that they had free power for life.

As I arrived in the city and stopped to pick up my friends, we came under fire again. I told the Celanas people that we are at a truce, and that the town was a free.

The Celanas kept firing and hitting our ship. Mark and I and the remaining humanoids got out and fired back until we ran the Celanas out of the city.

"I told you there would be trouble if you interfered," Mark said. "I think that you made the right decision for once. Now I understand what you mean by being free."

We went back into the Oakville tavern and told the people that the fight was between Loper's men and me and not the good people from there.

"From now on, your power is free," I said. "So don't let anyone try to charge you for electricity at all. We will drive them away. Now that you are free, I will bring the rest of my family here to have fun and to shop."

I told Satar and Tara about the Thine people and about how they had shot Doreen.

"Yes, and we are also friends," I said.

"I would love for you to come and visit, but be careful, Orian."

"Okay, my friend, but you better keep an eye out for this city to ensure its freedom."

"I will. I promise you that."

We all got into the starship. I made a pass around the city, searching for more of Loper's men. They seemed to have gone home for the moment.

I knew that there would be more fights on the planet, but I couldn't wait until I could enter the Thine peoples' world and explore their planet more.

Chapter Twelve

We had been on this planet for about a year in earth time now, but the time on the planet has been recorded as only about four weeks, because of the way our new planet moves around the suns. Doreen and I had doubts about the power plant that I had put on Loper's planet. I knew that it made a lot of people happy; they were in the city getting free energy and not having to pay Loper. I would go back there in a couple days, which would be about a month in Loper's world, and see how things were progressing with the new processing plant and how Loper was responding to the free energy. I gave him a choice to have us build him a complete power plant that would power his whole planet for easy charge and a very low price for the new energy. I was just waiting to see if he would take the offer.

My friends and I were still laughing at all the different aliens we had found so far and how funny looking they were. But we might look funny to them to as well. Today, I and a few others would enter a fourth world and see what that new planet was all about. This planet was called Dipha.

The creatures we had met from Dipha were funny looking bugs that walked on four feet, and their feet looked like hands except for the back feet, which looked like they could stand upright and look like overgrown cockroaches. We had to have the computer analyze their language so we could speak to them. Once the language had been analyzed, we could now hear their speech instead of having to use sign language.

They gave us permission to enter their portal, so I asked Doreen and the rest of the crew if they would like to come with us to visit this new world.

"Of course," Luke said, and as usual, he was ready to go; Luke was always ready for an adventure. Doreen, Amanda, and Beth decided that they would stay home to work around the house and make a few changes both in the house and throughout the big garden, which was growing so fast that we couldn't keep up with the canning process.

Luke, Shane, and I would take the largest spaceship and about twenty humanoids to go explore this new world and see what we could find. We got the ship ready to go and got all the humanoids into the ship; I had Mark sit beside me; my humanoid seemed to be in touch with everything I did. Luke sat in the back along with Shane. All of our small starships were special. They could fly through the air at lightspeed if needed. We also had the latest in weapon technology that would be sure to ward off any alien attacks.

We opened the shuttle bay and headed for the fourth world, a planet called Dipha. I would have to see if I could find Himbe, the head of the Thine people, whom I had seen when Himbe and his people were going to the source.

Off we flew in our nice spaceship. We headed for the unknown portal, anxious to see what was there. We got into this new world through the portal, and then we saw a very lush tropical world. There were all kinds of creatures that scurried about the base of a forest.

I thought to myself and then asked Mark, "How do you think we can find Himbe in these lush green forests?"

"Fly high over the canopy until we find a bug," Mark said.

As I looked down, I saw dog-like creatures that had jaws like an alligator's, other animals with wings, and a giant dinosaur-looking creature.

"I think this will be a hostile world," I said, as I looked down through the canopy. In the top of the canopy were snakelike creatures, and they had foot-long, slender bodies. We could see their large tongues trying to reach out and try to grab our starship.

"Why don't we fly around this planet really quickly and see if the whole planet is all forest or not," Mark said.

"Let's go," I said, and we set the starship at a nice speed to circle planet.

I had Mark send up some satellites as we traveled around Dipha. I decided that I was going to have to find a way to be able to broadcast signals through the portals so the computer could get signals from all the satellites that I put around each planet. That would, I think, keep an eye on the activity going on in each world.

As we traveled around the planet, we found that the temperature of the new world was around ninety-nine degrees Fahrenheit. I thought that was the cause for all the fog we saw in the forests around the planet. We looked for creatures that looked like Himbe, but hadn't found any as yet. As we circled the planet, we got readings of the air quality and other strange things that the sensors were picking up. The computer would have to compute these readings when we got back to home base.

As we got back close to the portal opening, which I had left open, we found an open area to land. We slowly went downward with the spaceship. Then Luke, Shane, and I got out, and we asked the humanoids to get out the rods and create a force field for the future to make a home to study this new world. The humanoids finished putting up the force fields. We had to be ready for anything on this planet.

We entered the forest. It was just beautiful. The animals were not scared of us, but some scratched their feet on the ground as if they were going to attack. There were huge, spider-like creatures crawling all over the place and a lot of animals that looked like dinosaurs. We tried communicating with some, but they didn't seem to have the brain power or the ability to speak. I guessed I should have paid more attention to Himbe. Some of the creatures were getting too close for comfort; they were as curious about us as we were about them.

We found out that the planet was very suitable for sustaining life if only we could make the portal hole bigger to let us bring our huge starship in and start a new life here. But I knew that would make Doreen mad. Doreen was the one who liked where we were already. She had built us a beautiful home, and Beth and Amanda had done a great job working in the garden and getting the cattle and hogs and chickens to full-grown size and grazing in the nice field that Shane had prepared.

We came in contact with a very large creature that had a bad attitude. The creature looked something like a huge T. rex with two heads. Then the creature started charging at us. We just stood still until creature got closer. He was huge. He stood upright and had jaws like a whale shark. He had his head down as he charged forward. We took out our hand phasers and started to shoot at him, but with the phasers in stun mode, the creature shrugged it off. So we set our phasers on high, and then shot the creature. That did the trick, and down he went. The creature dropped only six feet from us.

"Are there any rooms in the ship's cargo bay that will hold this larger creature?" I asked.

"Yes, Orian," Mark said.

I told Mark that I would like to take him home to see if he was any good to eat. Mark said yes, so I asked the humanoids to load the huge creature into the cargo bay of the ship.

We walked through the jungle. We went further in, and we kind of walked in between all these strange creatures with our eyes open for any aggression that the creatures might have against us.

As we went deeper and deeper into the jungle, the brush got so thick that we had to set our phasers to a laser light beam and make a pathway through the jungle. It wasn't a pleasant experience. There were mosquitoes the size of bats, and they were all trying to land on us and suck our blood. We put our force fields on high to keep them from penetrating our skin. I asked Mark to take some samples of some creatures that we had encountered.

"Why, Orian?" Mark asked.

"Mark, I would just like to check out their DNA," I said.

"Why?" Mark asked. I told Mark to forget what I'd just told him; he was right. But I did want to taste the meat from the creature that we had destroyed.

The canopy of the forest was so thick that we couldn't see the sky, so I told everyone to get ready to leave the world for the moment and to load everything and everyone back into the spaceship to get ready to go home.

When we were in our spaceship and had taken off for back home, I recalled that while traveling around the planet I had noticed it had four moons and one huge sun. *How beautiful,* I had thought.

"Would these trees in the forest be suitable for lumber for us to build something in wood in our new home," I asked Mark.

"Yes," Mark said.

"Let's go back to our world since we cannot find Himbe," I said to the crew. I went on to say, "We will send our mining equipment to lug some of these trees out to make space for a base camp here, and then maybe Himbe will come to us. But I would like to find out more about these creatures."

When we all arrived home, I decided I would go to Satar and Tara's world to visit them and see how the plants and trees were growing on their devastated planet. We flew into Satar and Tara's world, and we decided that we would talk to the Leamarkes and maybe show some of them the new world we found to see if they would like to live where there were a lot of large trees and vegetation, where they would make their nests high in the canopy.

Both Satar and Tara were together, so I landed our spacecraft and got out. I was greeted by Satar and Tara, and we all said hello. They invited me to dinner, along with Luke and Shane. Of course, we said yes. They told us that food was getting short there because of all of the destruction from the Vipeters. They had destroyed all the crops and most of the forest before they were destroyed in the large battle.

I told Satar and Tara about the new and fourth world that we had been to and that there was plenty of food there that was growing wild all over the world. They wanted to know more, so I talked about the large canopies. I said that the soil looked rich and could grow good crops. The only setback for our seeds was that the temperature was around ninety-nine degrees, and I wondered if our plants could take that kind of heat.

Satar said yes, and so did Tara, but they didn't want to really leave their world.

I asked Satar and Tara if we could help build the water system soon.

"Do you mind if humanoids do most of the work?" I asked.

"No," Satar said. "That would be fine. We would really appreciate that."

I asked Satar if we could take material from their planet to get some ore for our storage to build atoms. "That way, we can make the equipment that the humanoids need to build a canal system and to be able to plant more trees and crops in the desert area," I said. I told Satar and Tara that we had seen, from high above their planet, that there used to be water all over the desert area many years before.

"Our ancestors don't remember that," they said.

"The satellites even showed us that there were rivers and streams that once flowed through the desert," I said. "Would you like to go to the new world and see what I am talking about?" I asked Satar and Tara.

"Yes," they said.

"I will stop at the starship first and tell the computer about our plans for your world," I said. "But in the meantime," I told Satar and Tara, "you might like to live in this world that I'm about to show you. You might want to live there until things grow back on your planet."

The ship was overloaded so when we got back to the starship, I left most of the humanoids there and unloaded the large beast to be tested for meat to see if we could eat it. If we could eat it, then there would be plenty for us to eat, and we could hunt in Dipha to last us a lifetime. Mark also told the humanoids what to do on planet Dipha; we needed a home base on Dipha to do exploring there.

I took Satar and Tara to the new planet and flew them around the area, showing them all the berries and tall trees that were there that could sustain life. Satar and Tara liked the place, but they were concerned about all of creatures that were there and whether they would interfere with their lifestyle.

After some time on the planet, we still hadn't seen Himbe, but I was sure he would see our new base and be concerned about it and contact us. I would leave the portal open, and if some beasts came into our world, we would see how they would adapt. I didn't think our world would be suitable for the creatures; they would return to their world.

As we were getting ready to leave, we saw the first signs of mining equipment coming into the world, and humanoids started to make the base camp.

I took Satar and Tara and the rest of Leamarkes and Anomies back to their home planet, and they promised to leave the portal open to see if more insects and birds flying to their planet might start to nest. Our bird population might expand to eventually have animals from Earth roaming the planets.

When I got home, I dropped off Luke and Shane and told twenty-five humanoids to get into the starship.

"We are going to fly to Loper's planet to see how the power supply is working," I said.

As the humanoids loaded into the ship, I thought to myself, *Someday, I will have to name all these humanoids.*

I went into the starship to where all the weapons were and grabbed a new gun that the computer had made for me, just in case I got in trouble on Loper's planet. The gun was sleek and had about a three-inch barrel with a lot of controls down by the handle of the gun. The computer helped me understand how to use the weapon, from the stun phase to the killing phase. The computer also had me put on a new belt that would adjust the force field in case I found some kind of new weapon technology that I might encounter.

I flew off in my starship to Loper's planet to see how things were going with the new power plant. As soon as I entered, my ship came under fire and was attacked by the Celanas people. I noticed that there were hundreds of Celanas all throughout the city, destroying everything. The city was as dark as dark could be. There were no more beautiful lights to be seen in the sky or in the city itself. I noticed that the Celanas people were killing innocent aliens in the streets as I was being attacked. I started to fire back, with my gun set to kill. My new weapons did decisive damage to the Celanas.

I landed in front of Lepkwod's bar and entertainment center to find out what was going on. As I landed, I asked the humanoids to fire upon the Celanas people and try to get them to stop killing all the nice aliens that were in the city. I was furious.

Then I got out of the starship. I was being shot at, so I brought out my big gun and shot back to destroy the Celanas people one by one.

"Where is Loper?" I yelled. "I would like to speak to him. Stop your fighting!"

I walked into Lepkwod's place and found him lying on the floor, badly hurt. I asked Mark to help me put Lepkwod on the bar. We lifted him off the floor, put him on the bar, and started to bandage his wounds. He was terribly hurt, but he was still in a good mood as always.

"What happened?" I asked.

"Where were you guys?" he asked.

"All you had to do was come and get us, and we would have helped right away," I said.

"Loper changed the code on the portal so we couldn't get out to get help," he said.

"Is there a doctor around?" I asked.

"Yes," Lepkwod said. "He lives across the street if he is still alive."

"Go get him," I said to Mark. "I will watch over Lepkwod's place in the city of Minatar."

Mark went to get the doctor, and I got Lepkwod something to drink and asked him more questions.

"Why are Loper's men attacking the city?" I asked.

"It's all because of the new power plant," Lepkwod said. "Loper didn't like us getting free energy, so he cut the cables that go to our cities and came in and threatened to charge us the same price for electricity, even though you said it was free."

"Yes, that is what I told you, Lepkwod, and your people, and I will make sure that Loper understands that he can't control all power in this world." I thought, *What kind of a man is Loper to do these things?*

I heard the humanoids shooting. Some of the humanoids' force fields were getting lower as the Celanas people were constantly firing at them. I went out the door and told the humanoids to stand behind the starship and recharge. But that didn't do any good, because they were being shot at from every direction. I told the humanoids to get into the spaceship to be protected by the starship's force field while their force fields charged up. Then the Celanas were in position to shoot at Lepkwod and me.

Soon Mark came across the street with the doctor and protected him with his force field. I told Mark to set up a force field in front of Lepkwod's establishment, so Mark hurried and set up a defense shield in front of Lepkwod's place.

As the doctor worked on Lepkwod, he told me that we should not have interfered, even though they were getting cheated when paying for electricity. I told the doctor, whose name was Cillin, that I would take care of everything, even if I had to destroy all of the Celanas.

"So many have died already," Cillin said, "and we really don't want to have more die just to have electricity."

The force fields were holding at Lepkwod's place, so I told Mark to get into the starship.

"Let's stop some of the violence and reconnect electricity to the city and others," I said.

Mark and I got into the starship, and as we rose, the starship was getting fired upon from all directions. I noticed that the force field was down to 80 percent. I was a little concerned, but I told Mark, "Let's go."

The first thing we did was go to Loper's main power plant. When we arrived, we shot five lazerpon torpedoes at Loper's power plant. The first torpedo failed, but the second torpedo made a dent in the plant's defenses. The third torpedo struck the building, and a huge explosion took place. The fifth lazerpon torpedo wiped out the entire plant. The whole planet went dark while plenty of Celanas people were firing upon us. Our force fields were getting weaker.

I got on the speakerphone and asked to speak to Loper.

"Loper is dead," said one the Celanas.

"Then who is in charge?" I asked.

"I am," said a man named Bulus, yelling with an angry voice.

"We need to talk," I said to Bulus.

"There is nothing to talk about," Bulus said. "We will destroy the city. Then we are going to your world to destroy you."

"Good luck," I said.

Mark and I took off high into the atmosphere to recharge. We came close to the portal to make sure it was open. We made a call to Luke and Shane and told them to gather humanoids and several starships and to come join us in a fight. We needed at least fifty starships and a thousand humanoids. Luke was excited; he liked a good fight. Shane was nervous, but he said he would come as well. I asked the computer to analyze our force fields and the damage that had been done to them and if the computer could reconfigure our force fields to be able to withstand the Celanas' new guns.

The Celanas people and Bulus had huge machinery with large cannons that shot strong laser beams at us and at the people in the city, destroying buildings and killing more aliens. As we flew around, we saw the alien town where the Celanas people lived, and we open fire on their city, destroying buildings and killing their people. We almost completely wiped out the entire city. They didn't have much defense around the city, because they had thought it would be hard to detect.

Well, word got out to Bulus what we had done, and it made Bulus even more furious. Bulus took this huge army through the city, destroying everything in sight. We fought back, destroying some of the machinery. Our ship got hit by the strong laser beam. It shook our ship and did some damage to our force fields.

"Computer, can you reconfigure our force field?" I asked.

Mark told me that the computer would have to take some time to analyze the new weapons that had been developed by Loper after he'd watching us fight when we'd fought together to help Tara and Satar.

Pretty soon, Luke and several starships came through the portal and opened fire on the Celanas. The starships were taking hits from the large cannons that the Celanas starships had. There were hundreds of ships, and we didn't know if we could hold out. I asked Mark to tell the computer to make more starships so we could be even in the fight.

The starships started to fly through the portal and head toward our home and our big starship. Mark told the computer to be ready and to put the force fields on full strength. He told the computer to have all the guns of the starship ready to fire on the enemy.

One of our starships got shot so many times that it finally blew up in a big explosion right in front of us. Fortunately, it was flown by a humanoid and not by Luke or Shane. I told all the starships to fly through the portal and go around the planet our world. They needed to recharge and then come back at full strength to fight the aliens. Our starships fought furiously, shooting at the crafts the aliens were using to shoot at us.

I told all starships to switch to lazerpon torpedoes and see if that would work. The starships locked on to each craft that the aliens had and fired upon their crafts with lazerpon torpedoes. The first torpedo did no damage; the second one did some damage; the third one blew up the crafts. They were doing extensive damage to us as well.

We blew up at least fifty of their crafts, and we lost a total of five starships.

One starship that was badly damaged was Luke's, and he was hurt.

"Fly back to the shuttle bay and get the medical attention," I told him.

The computer was working hard to create more starships and humanoids to fight the oncoming threat.

As I was battling oncoming crafts, I took a couple of direct hits to the back of my ship, and suddenly, there was damage to the engine. I headed straight for the starship with my spacecraft, struggling to keep in flight. I worked hard at the controls as I continued to get hit by the alien crafts' guns. I got a piece of scrap metal in my arm, and I knew that I had to get to sick bay. I finally flew in through the starship's force field and made a crash landing in the starship's shuttle bay. I asked the computer to restart or repair the spacecraft; I wanted my spacecraft fixed right away.

"Why were the force fields not restored after the first few hits?" I asked the computer.

"This is a new kind of gun and laser that I have never come across before," the computer said. "I am doing the best I can to compute how to restore your force fields to withstand these laser hits on your ships."

The spacecraft that was at the other end of the planet started to come back in and engage in the fighting with the Celanas spacecrafts. They used lazerpon torpedoes to make direct hits on the Celanas spacecrafts.

"That spacecraft and the force field are all down to eighty-five percent," Mark said.

The starship's guns were firing laser beams at the oncoming crafts, destroying a good percentage of them as they attacked our ship. We were doing a lot of damage to the spacecrafts that Bulus had sent after us. But it wasn't enough, because Bulus had many crafts; they outnumbered ours ten to one. We didn't know if we would hold our ground as their spacecrafts kept shooting at our defenses.

I told Doreen, Beth, and Amanda to get into the starship for protection. The main starship guns were doing more damage to the spacecrafts than our guns on our smaller starships were doing. I thought the main starship could hold its own against incoming enemy, but I didn't know if the force field around our home outside would hold.

In between all the fighting, I asked the computer to make a huge Taperian force erupter for the poor for the entire planet of Saphra.

"It might take two days to create such an erupter," the computer said. Then I asked if my starship was repaired, and the computer said, "No. It will take a couple of days, because I am making more spacecrafts to fight the aliens."

"Computer," I asked, "do you have another ship available for me that will help protect me from the blasts of Bulus's spacecrafts?"

"Yes, I built one more for you, Orian, and I have finally completed the new reconfiguration for the force fields too."

"Mark," I asked, "can you put one of the guns like the starship has on my new spacecraft?"

"Yes, I can," Mark said. "Just give me a few minutes."

I told Luke and Shane that I had to go back to talk to Bulus about putting in a new power plant and to try to make peace. But Bulus was mad that we had attacked the city that the Celanas lived in. It was my fault that I had killed women and children, like the Celanas people were doing in the city of Minatar, but I guessed that was war.

The force field started to strengthen around the home again along with our defenses in the starship. Then all of a sudden, there came a second wave of Bulus's spacecrafts. They started shooting stronger lasers at our home and at our big starship. The huge starship fired massive guns at the oncoming spacecrafts and was doing a lot of damage to Bulus's army.

Then I saw in the distance, thousands of men armed with guns heading our way from on top of the starship. I asked the computer and Mark if we fire could from this distance to help protect the ship and our home. The computer said yes. Then our starship pointed some of its guns at the oncoming army.

Luke was still in sick bay, getting his wounds fixed when I asked Shane and the humanoids to arm up and get in position to hold the army back. We all put our force fields on full and headed out into the field around the spacecrafts with guns blazing from the main starship and shooting down some of the spacecrafts of the Celanas. That helped keep us from being shot at from above. Our spacecrafts were intertwined with their spacecrafts as the battle continued. Some of our starships got destroyed, along with the humanoids flying them, but we also shot down many of Bulus's spacecrafts as well.

Mark had told me when I put in that new power plant that this might happen, but I had not thought it was start a war with innocent aliens getting killed and our starship and home being at risk.

As the alien army closed in on us, the aliens took positions and started firing. Their laser beams were strong. Some of the mushroom trees were hit, and they toppled over. We fired back, and our phasers did some damage but not as much as their stronger lasers. The computer tried to analyze their laser beams to see if our phasers could be upgraded. Mark said that the computer was working on it and that we would hold our ground. I told Shane to go back inside with the girls and Luke.

"This is my fight," I said. "I started this, and I don't want to see anything happen to you guys."

Bulus's army was coming closer, and laser beams were hitting our home but not fazing the starship. I looked up in the air and saw that the starships were doing damage to the spacecrafts of the Celanas people, but we were also getting destroyed. We were down to only about thirty spacecrafts.

I yelled at the army leader and said, "Let me talk to Bulus."

"I am here," Bulus said.

"There has been enough blood spilt today," I said. "Can I talk to you about peace?"

"No," Bulus said.

I told Bulus that I had been going to build a power plant for Loper, and he had agreed that free electricity could make money and help clean up the environment.

"I am not Loper," Bulus said, "and I make the decisions now."

"Then how are we going to make peace?" I yelled.

"We will destroy you and your spacecrafts so you don't interfere anymore in our business," Bulus said.

I sent a couple of humanoids to ask Tara and Satar to help us in the fight, and I also sent a couple humanoids to planet Zipam to find out from Sanfe if there was anybody who would help us fight the Celanas in our world. I asked the humanoid to tell him that we were in turmoil right then.

Meanwhile, the humanoids and I were fighting the alien army. Some of the humanoids next to me got hit by Bulus's phasers and laser weapons and were destroyed. Several of my humanoids were lost, and the force fields around our home were starting to fail. I asked Mark to tell the computer to upgrade the force fields and put more power into the system. The computer told Mark that it would put 100 percent more power into the defense system around the house and the entire defense system around the crop area as well. That brought our defense shields to around 95 percent. I also asked Mark, who was slightly wounded, to ask our computer to increase our force fields.

"The computer is trying," Mark said. "But it is straining with all the power that is put around the defenses outside, so we should take our people inside our own perimeter."

I told the humanoids to retreat back to the settlement where we would set up laser cannons to keep in combat mode with the attacking army. The humanoids that were inside the perimeter had already set up laser cannons, which were shooting Lazerpon torpedoes. As soon as Mark and the humanoids got back into the perimeter, we manned the cannons and shot Lazerpon torpedoes at the surrounding army.

A lot of Celanas were being destroyed, and it looked like victory was at hand, when out of the blue, more spacecrafts appeared and started shooting at our defenses. Our starships were in the shuttle bay getting repaired, so we were defenseless in the air, but with our laser cannons, we would lock onto the spacecrafts and shoot. We were shooting in all directions. Our force fields around our home started to fail, and then the home got hit hard. Part of the roof and the interior were destroyed.

We continued to fight hard, but as our defenses weakened and their lasers penetrated our perimeter, I got hit in the arm and was bleeding badly. Mark put a towel over my wound and tied a knot tightly to stop the bleeding. It hurt like hell, but I bit my teeth and fought on as we killed Bulus's army.

As bleak as it looked for us, we knew that, if we all retreated to the main starship, we would be safe. Starship guns kept firing and knocking crafts out of the sky. In some ways, we were winning, and in other ways, we were losing.

"How many people must die now?" I yelled to Bulus.

"The way it looks to me," Bulus said, "it looks like you will be the ones who will die."

"I want peace, Bulus, and I told you I'd build you a free power plant that would supply your world with all the power needed for free, and you can charge a small fee for power that people could afford."

"This is not about power, it is about you interfering with our planet," Bulus said.

I told Bulus that he was a dictator, and that dictating what people should have to pay is not a way of life. "Bulus, you keep attacking us. We will adapt and come back and destroy you."

Then we retreated into the ship as our defenses were overrun. They damaged our garden and destroyed our house. They could not destroy the starship; the starship was too powerful. Our starship's laser cannons kept firing on.

"Bulus," I yelled from the starships loudspeakers, "you will never win. As we speak, your weapons are being analyzed by our computer system and, eventually, will be rendered useless against us."

The humanoids with Satar and Tara did not return, because Bulus's army was around the starship, firing constantly at the ship. Even though we were fighting back and destroying many of Bulus's army, they still kept advancing. There seemed to be more and more Celanas coming toward our ship. I had not realized the number of people that the Celanas had.

As I sat and watched our house being destroyed, I was getting very depressed. I knew we were safer in the starship, but all at work that Doreen and Amanda and Beth and Shane had done was being destroyed.

Then all of a sudden, several different kinds of ships of all shapes and sizes joined the fight against the Celanas people. They had laser cannons. They had torpedoes, and they came in force with hundreds of ships of all kinds. They must have come from planet Zipam, I thought. Sure enough, they did. I got a call from Sanfe. He said he had gone to the city and mustered up all of the aliens that were in the city to see if they wanted to fight in a tremendous battle that was going on in our world. Of course, those aliens loved to fight.

As Bulus saw all the ships and how they were destroying his people and his ships, he headed back toward the portal. Soon, they were out of our area. Most of their men were dead. Sanfe had saved the day. I told Sanfe to thank everyone.

"When I come to planet Zipam, I will buy them all drinks and thank them in person, but for now, we have to repair what has been destroyed," I said.

"You're welcome," Sanfe said. "Orian, any time you need help, just call us."

"Thanks, Sanfe," I said. "And tell all your friends thank you."

The battle finally ended, and we had gotten a terrible beating. But because we had made friends in different worlds, we were able to beat our enemies, and I would rebuild all that was damaged. When the new Taperian force erupter was ready, I would give power back to Bulus's planet and have it run by the people and not by the Celanas people. I would do that soon.

I couldn't wait to explore what was through all the rest of the portals and to explore the different worlds that they might hold.

About the Author

My name is Michael Jesweak. I was born in 1954. I come from a small town called Cadillac in Michigan. I finished high school in 1972 and started working as a mason. I did some farming. Later in life, I was a full-time farmer, and I raised livestock and field crops. I sold my farm sometime in the 1990s and moved to Port Charlotte, Florida, with my children.

I went back to college, and I received degrees in computer science and networking. During my English classes, I excelled in creative writing; I did not excel in grammar. At that time, I didn't think of writing a book. I think now I have found my true dream in life: to be an author of an exciting book.

I hope that my readers enjoy reading this book as much I enjoyed writing it.